Irish author **Abby Green** threw in a very glamorous
career in film and TV—which really consisted of a
lot of standing in the rain outside actors' trailers—to
pursue her love of romance. After she'd bombarded
Mills & Boon with manuscripts they kindly accepted one,
and an author was born. She lives in Dublin, Ireland, and
loves any excuse for distraction. Visit abby-green.com or
e-mail abbygreenauthor@gmail.com.

Visit the Author Profile page at
millsandboon.co.uk for more titles.

I'd like to thank Heidi Rice, Sharon Kendrick
and Iona Grey for all their cheerleading, Kate Meader,
who provided counsel over cocktails in the Shelbourne,
and Annie West, who always provides serene and
insightful advice. And of course my editor, Sheila,
who has proved beyond doubt that she believes me
capable of anything, apart from perhaps AWAVMOT!

Thank you all!

CLAIMED FOR THE DE CARRILLO TWINS

BY
ABBY GREEN

...ons and
...y real
...siness
...lance is

...by way of
...irculated
...inding or
...a similar
...bsequent

...rk owner
...red with the
...onisation in
the Internal Market and in other countries.

First Published in Great Britain 2017
By Mills & Boon, an imprint of HarperCollins*Publishers*
1 London Bridge Street, London, SE1 9GF

© 2017 Abby Green

ISBN: 978-0-263-92404-6

PROLOGUE

CRUZ DE CARRILLO SURVEYED the thronged reception room in his London home, filled with a veritable who's who of London's most powerful players and beautiful people, all there to celebrate his return to Europe.

He felt no sense of accomplishment, though, to be riding high on the crest of his stratospheric success in North America, having tripled his eponymous bank's fortunes in less than a year, because he knew his zealous focus on work had more to do with avoiding *this* than the burning ambition he'd harboured for years to turn his family bank's fortune and reputation around.

And it killed him to admit it.

This was standing just feet away from him now—tall and slender, yet with generous curves. Pale skin. Too much pale skin. Exposed in a dress that left far too little to the imagination. Cruz's mouth compressed with distaste even as his blood ran hot, mocking him for the desire which time hadn't diminished—much to his intense irritation. It was unwelcome and completely inappropriate. Now more than ever. She was his sister-in-law.

Her blonde hair was up in a sleek chignon and a chain of glittering gold trailed tantalisingly down her naked back, bared in a daring royal blue backless dress. She turned slightly in Cruz's direction and he had to tense every muscle to stave off the surge of fresh desire when he saw the provocative curves of her high full breasts, barely disguised by the thin draped satin.

She looked almost vulnerable, set apart from the crowd slightly, but he knew that was just a mirage.

He cursed her. And he cursed himself. If he hadn't been

so weak he wouldn't know how incendiary it felt to have those curves pressed against his body. He wouldn't remember the way her eyes had turned a stormy dark blue as he'd plundered the sweetness she'd offered up to him that fateful night almost eighteen months ago, in this very house, when she'd worked for him as a housemaid.

He wouldn't still hear her soft, breathy moans in his dreams, forcing him awake, sweating, with his hand wrapped around himself and every part of him straining for release…aching to know the intimate clasp of her body, milking him into sweet oblivion.

Sweet. That was just it. There was nothing sweet about this woman. He might have thought so at one time—she'd used to blush if he so much as glanced at her—but it had all been an elaborate artifice. Because his younger half-brother, Rio, had told him the truth about what she really was, and she was no innocent.

Her seduction of Cruz had obviously been far more calculated than he'd believed, and when that hadn't worked she'd diverted her sights onto Rio, his illegitimate half-brother, with whom Cruz had a complicated relationship—to put it mildly.

A chasm had been forged between the brothers when they were children—when Cruz had been afforded every privilege as the legitimate heir to the De Carrillo fortune, and Rio, who had been born to a housemaid of the family *castillo*, had been afforded nothing. Not even the De Carrillo name.

But Cruz had never felt that Rio should be punished for their charismatic and far too handsome father's inability to control his base appetites. So he had done everything in his power after their father had died some ten years previously to make amends—going against their father's will, which had left Rio nothing, by becoming his guardian, giving him his rightful paternalistic name and paying for him to complete his education.

Then, when he had come of age, Cruz had given him a fair share of his inheritance *and* a job—first in the De Carrillo bank in Madrid, and now in London, much to the conservative board's displeasure.

At the age of twenty-one Rio had become one of Europe's newest millionaires, the centre of feverish media attention with his dark good looks and mysterious past. And he had lapped it up, displaying an appetite for the kind of playboy lifestyle Cruz had never indulged in, quickly marrying one of the world's top supermodels in a lavish wedding that had gone on for days—only for it to end in tragedy nearly a year later, when she'd died in an accident shortly after giving birth to twin boys.

And yet, much as Rio's full-throttle existence had unnerved Cruz, could he begrudge him that after being denied his heritage?

Cruz's conscience pricked. By giving Rio his due inheritance and his rightful name perhaps he'd made his brother a target for gold-diggers? Rio's first wife had certainly revelled in her husband's luxurious lifestyle, and it would appear as if nothing had changed with his second wife.

As if sensing his intense regard, his sister-in-law turned now and saw him. Her eyes widened and her cheeks flushed. Cruz's anger spiked. She could still turn it on. Even now. When he knew her real capabilities.

She faced him in that provocative dress and her luscious body filled his vision and made his blood thrum with need. He hated her for it. She moved towards him almost hesitantly, the slippery satin material moving sinuously around her long legs.

He called on every atom of control he had and schooled his body not to respond to her proximity even as her tantalising scent tickled his nostrils, threatening to weaken him all over again. It was all at once innocent, yet seductive. As if he needed reminding that she presented one face to the world while hiding another, far more mercenary one.

'Trinity.' His voice sounded unbearably curt to his ears, and he tried to ignore the striking light blue eyes. To ignore how lush her mouth was, adding a distinctly sensual edge to her pale blonde innocence.

An innocence that was skin-deep.

'Cruz...it's nice to see you again.'

Her voice was husky, reminding him vividly of how it had sounded in his ear that night. *'Please...'*

His dry tone disguised his banked rage. 'You've come up in the world since we last met.'

She swallowed, the long, delicate column of her pale throat moving. 'Wh-what do you mean?'

Cruz's jaw tightened at the faux innocence. 'I'm talking about your rapid ascent from the position of nanny to wife and stepmother to my nephews.'

That brought back the unwelcome reminder that he'd only been informed about the low-key wedding in a text from Rio.

I have you to thank for sending this beautiful woman into my life. I hope you'll be very happy for us, brother.

The news had precipitated shock, and something much darker into Cruz's gut. And yet he hadn't had any reason at that point not to believe it was a good idea—in spite of his own previous experience with Trinity, which he'd blamed himself for. Rio had been a widower, and he and Trinity had obviously forged a bond based on caring for his nephews. Cruz had believed that she was a million light years away from Rio's glamorous hedonistic first wife. *Then.*

The fact that he'd had dreams for weeks afterwards,

of being held back and forced to watch a faceless blonde woman making love to countless men, was something that made him burn inwardly with shame even now.

Trinity looked pale. Hesitant. 'I was looking for you, actually. Could we have a private word?'

Cruz crushed the unwelcome memory and arched a brow. 'A private word?'

He flicked a glance at the crowd behind her and then looked back to her, wondering what the hell she was up to. Surely she wouldn't have the gall to try and seduce him under the same roof she had before, with her husband just feet away?

'We're private enough here. No one is listening.'

She flushed and then glanced behind her and back, clearly reluctant. 'Perhaps this isn't the best time or place...'

So he'd been right. Disgust settled in his belly. 'Spit it out, Trinity. Unless it's not *talking* you're interested in.'

She blanched, and that delicate flush disappeared. Once her ability to display emotions had intrigued him. Now it incensed him.

'What do you mean?'

'You know very well what I mean. You tried to seduce me in this very house, and when it didn't work you transferred your attentions to my brother. He obviously proved to be more susceptible to your wiles.'

She shook her head and frowned, a visibly trembling hand coming up to her chest as if to contain shock, disbelief. 'I don't know what you're talking about...'

Disgust filled Cruz that she could stand here and so blatantly lie while her enormous rock of an engagement ring glinted at him mockingly. All he could see was her and her treachery. But he had to crush the recriminations that rose up inside him—it was too late for them now.

Rio had revealed to Cruz on his return to the UK a

few days before that he was on the verge of bankruptcy—his huge inheritance all but wiped out. And Trinity De Carrillo's name was all over nearly every receipt and docket that had led his brother further and further into the mire. The extent of how badly Cruz had misread her was galling.

An insidious thought occurred to him and it made his blood boil. 'Your innocent act is past its sell-by date. I might not have realised what you were up to—more fool me—but I know now. Rio has told me how you've single-handedly run through almost every cent he has to his name in a bid to satisfy your greedy nature. Now you're realising his fortune isn't a bottomless pit, perhaps you're looking for a way out, or even a new benefactor?'

Before she could respond he continued in a low, bitter voice.

'I underestimated your capacity to play the long game, Trinity. You lulled Rio into a false sense of trust by manipulating his biggest vulnerability—his sons. I'm very well aware of how my actions pushed you in the direction of my brother, and that is not something I will ever forgive myself for. Needless to say if he requires financial help he will receive it, but your days of bankrupting him are over. If you're hoping to bargain your way out of this predicament then think again. You'll get no sympathy from me.'

Trinity was so white now Cruz fancied he could see the blood vessels under her skin. A part of him wished she would break out of character and get angry with him for confronting her with who she really was.

Her hand dropped back to her side and she shook her head. 'You have it all wrong.'

'That's the best you can come up with?' he sneered. 'I have it *all wrong*? If I "have it all wrong" then, please, tell me what you want to discuss.'

Cruz could see the pulse at the base of her neck beating hectically. His own pulse-rate doubled.

'I wanted to talk to you about Rio...about his behaviour. It's been growing more and more erratic... I'm worried about the boys.'

Cruz let out a short, incredulous laugh. 'Worried about the boys? You're really trying to play the concerned stepmother card in a bid to deflect attention from the fact that you're more concerned about your lavish lifestyle coming to an end?'

Bitterness filled Cruz. He knew better than most how the biological bond of a parent and child didn't guarantee love and security. Far from it.

'You're not even related to them—you've just used them as pawns to manipulate your way into my brother's bed and get a ring on your finger.'

Trinity took a step back, her eyes wide with feigned shock. He had to hand it to her. She was a good actress.

Almost as if she was talking to herself now, she said, 'I should have known he'd protect himself somehow...of course you'd believe him over me.'

A sliver of unease pierced Cruz's anger but he pushed it aside. 'I've known Rio all of his twenty-five years. I think it's safe to say I'd trust my own flesh and blood over a conniving gold-digger any day of the week.'

Heated colour came back into Trinity's cheeks. She looked at him, big blue eyes beseeching him with commendable authenticity.

'I'm not a gold-digger. You don't understand. Everything you're saying is all wrong—my marriage with Rio is not what you—'

'*There* you are, darling. I've been looking for you. Charlotte Lacey wants to talk to you about next week's charity function.'

Cruz blanched. He hadn't even noticed Rio joining

them. He'd been consumed with the woman in front of him, whose arm was now being taken firmly in her husband's hand. Rio's dark brown eyes met Cruz's over Trinity's head. They were hard. Trinity had gone even paler, if that was possible.

'If you don't mind, brother, I need to steal my wife away.'

Cruz could see it in Rio's eyes then—a familiar resentment. And shame and anger. Futility choked him. There was nothing he could do. He knew Rio would already be despising the fact that he'd allowed Cruz to see him brought so low at this woman's greedy hands.

He watched as they walked back into the crowd, and it wasn't long before they left for the evening—without saying goodbye. Rio might have shown Cruz a chink of vulnerability by revealing his financial problems, but if anything that only demonstrated how much Trinity had got to him—because he'd never before allowed his brother to see a moment's weakness. Cruz's sense that his determination to see Rio treated fairly had been futile rose up again—he had never truly bridged the gap between them.

Cruz stood at the window in his drawing room and watched his brother handing Trinity into the passenger seat of a dark Jeep in the forecourt outside the house, before he got into the driver's seat himself.

He felt grim. All he could do now was be there to pick up the pieces of Rio's financial meltdown and do his best to ensure that Rio got a chance to start again—and that his wife didn't get her grasping hands on another cent.

At the last second, as if hearing his thoughts, Trinity turned her head to look at Cruz through the ground-floor window. For a fleeting moment their eyes met, and he could have sworn he saw hers shimmer with moisture, even from this distance.

He told himself they had to be tears of anger now that

she knew she'd been found out. She was trapped in a situation of her own making. It should have filled Cruz with a sense of satisfaction, but instead all he felt was a heavy weight in his chest.

Rio's Jeep took off with a spurt of gravel.

Cruz didn't realise it then, but it would be the last time he saw his brother alive.

CHAPTER ONE

Three months later. Solicitor's office.

TRINITY'S HEART STOPPED and her mouth dried. 'Mr De Carrillo is joining us?'

The solicitor glanced at her distractedly, looking for a paper on his overcrowded desktop. 'Yes—he is the executor of his brother's will, and we *are* in his building,' he pointed out redundantly.

She'd been acutely aware that she was in the impressive De Carrillo building in London's bustling financial zone, but it hadn't actually occurred to her that Cruz himself would be here.

To her shame, her first instinct was to check her appearance—which of course she couldn't do, but she was glad of the choice of clothing she'd made: dark loose trousers and a grey silk shirt. She'd tied her long hair back in a braid, as much out of habit when dealing with small energetic boys than for any other reason. She hadn't put on any make-up and regretted that now, fearing she must look about eighteen.

Just then there was a light knock on the door and it opened. She heard Mr Drew's assistant saying in a suspiciously breathless and awestruck voice, 'Mr De Carrillo, sir.'

The solicitor stood up, immediately obsequious, greeting Cruz De Carrillo effusively and leading him to a seat beside Trinity's on the other side of his desk.

Every nerve came to immediate and tingling life. The tiny hairs on her arms stood up, quivering. She lamented her uncontrollable reaction—would she ever *not* react to him?

She sensed him come to stand near her, tall and effortlessly intimidating. Childishly, she wanted to avoid looking at him. His scent was a tantalising mix of musk and something earthy and masculine. It was his scent now that sent her hurtling back to that cataclysmic evening in his house three months ago, when she'd realised just how badly Rio had betrayed her.

The shock of knowing that Rio obviously hadn't told him the truth about their marriage was still palpable, even now. And the fact that Cruz had so readily believed the worst of her hurt far worse than it should.

It had hurt almost as much as when he'd looked at her with dawning horror and self-disgust after kissing her to within an inch of her life. It was an experience still seared onto her brain, so deeply embedded inside her that she sometimes woke from X-rated dreams, tangled amongst her sheets and sweating. Almost two years later it was beyond humiliating.

Trinity dragged her mind away from that disturbing labyrinth of memories. She had more important things to deal with now. Because three months ago, while she and Rio had been driving home from Cruz's house, they'd been involved in a car crash and Rio had tragically died.

Since that day she'd become lone step-parent to Mateo and Sancho, Rio's two-and-a-half-year-old twins. Miraculously, she'd escaped from the accident with only cuts and bruises and a badly sprained ankle. She had no memory of the actual accident—only recalled waking in the hospital feeling battered all over and learning of her husband's death from a grim and ashen-faced Cruz.

Gathering her composure, she stood up to face him, steeling herself against his effect. Which was useless. As soon as she looked at him it was like a blow to her solar plexus.

She'd seen him since the night of the accident—at the

funeral, of course, and then when he'd called at the house for brief perfunctory visits to check that she and his nephews had everything they needed. He hadn't engaged with her beyond that. Her skin prickled now with foreboding. She had a sense that he'd merely been biding his time.

She forced herself to say, as calmly as she could, 'Cruz.'

'Trinity.'

His voice reverberated deep inside her, even as he oozed his habitual icy control.

The solicitor had gone back around his desk and said now, 'Espresso, wasn't it, Mr De Carrillo?'

Trinity blinked and looked to see the older gentleman holding out a small cup and saucer. Instinctively, because she was closer and because it was good manners, she reached for it to hand it to Cruz, only belatedly realising that her hand was trembling.

She prayed he wouldn't notice the tremor as she held out the delicate china to him. His hand was masculine and square. Strong. Long fingers…short, functional nails. At that moment she had a flash of remembering how his hand had felt between her legs, stroking her intimately…

Just before he took the cup and saucer there was a tiny clatter of porcelain on porcelain, evidence of her frayed nerves. *Damn*.

When he had the cup she sat down again quickly, before she made a complete fool of herself, and took a quick fortifying sip of her own cup of tea. He sat down too, and she was aware of his powerful body taking up a lot of space.

While Mr. Drew engaged Cruz De Carrillo in light conversation, before they started discussing the terms of Rio's will, Trinity risked another glance at the man just a couple of feet to her left.

Short dark blond hair gave more than a hint of his supremely controlled nature. Controlled except for that momentary lapse…an undoubtedly rare moment of heated insanity with someone he'd seen as far beneath him.

Trinity crushed the spike of emotion. She couldn't afford it.

Despite the urbane uniform of a three-piece suit, his impressive build was apparent. Muscles pushed at the fabric in a way that said he couldn't be contained, no matter how civilised he might look.

His face was a stunning portrait of masculine beauty, all hard lines and an aquiline profile that spoke of a pure and powerful bloodline. He had deep-set eyes and a mouth that on anyone else would have looked ridiculously sensual. Right now though, it looked stern. Disapproving.

Trinity realised that she was staring at him, and when he turned to look at her she went puce. She quickly turned back to the solicitor, who had stopped talking and was now looking from her to Cruz nervously, as if he could sense the tension in the room.

He cleared his throat. 'As you're both here now, I see no reason not to start.'

'If you would be so kind.'

Trinity shivered at the barely veiled impatience in Cruz's voice. She could recall only too well how this man had reduced grown men and women to quivering wrecks with just a disdainful look from those glittering dark amber eyes.

The half-brothers hadn't been very alike—where Rio had been dark, with obsidian eyes and dark hair, Cruz possessed a cold, tawny beauty that had always made Trinity think of dark ice over simmering heat. She shivered… she'd felt that heat.

'Mrs De Carrillo…?'

Trinity blinked and flushed at being caught out again. The solicitor's impatient expression came into focus. He was holding out a sheaf of papers and she reached for them.

'I'm sorry.' It still felt weird to be called Mrs De Carrillo—it wasn't as if she'd ever *really* been Rio's wife.

She quickly read the heading: *Last will and testament of Rio De Carrillo*. Her heart squeezed as she thought of the fact that Mateo and Sancho had now lost both their parents, too prematurely.

As bitter as her experience had been with Rio in the end, after Trinity had been sickened to realise just how manipulative he'd been, and how naive she'd been, she'd never in a million years have wished him gone.

She'd felt a level of grief that had surprised her, considering the fact that their marriage had been in name only—for the convenience of having a steady mother figure for the boys and because Rio had wanted to promote a more settled image to further his own ambitions.

Trinity had agreed to the union for those and myriad other reasons—the most compelling of which had to do with her bond with the twins, which had been forged almost as soon as she'd seen them. Two one-year-old cherubs, with dark hair, dark mischievous eyes and heart-stopping smiles.

Her heart had gone out to them because they were motherless, as she had been since she was a baby, and they'd latched on to her with a ferocity that she hadn't been able to resist, even though she'd known it would be more professional to try and keep some distance.

She'd also agreed because Rio's sad personal story—he had been all but abandoned by his own parents—had again chimed with echoes of her own. And because he'd agreed to help her fulfil her deepest ambitions—to go to university and get a degree, thereby putting her in a position to forge her own future, free of the stain of her ignominious past.

Rio hadn't revealed the full extent of *his* ambitions until shortly before the accident—and that was when she'd realised why he'd taken such perverse pleasure in marrying her. It had had far more to do with his long-held simmering resentment towards his older half-brother than any real desire to forge a sense of security for his sons, or to shake off his playboy moniker...

The solicitor was speaking. 'As you'll see, it's a relatively short document. There's really no need to read through it all now. Suffice to say that Mr De Carrillo bequeathed everything to his sons, Mateo and Sancho, and he named you their legal guardian, Trinity.'

She looked up. She'd known that Rio had named her guardian. Any concerns she'd had at the time, contemplating such a huge responsibility had been eclipsed by the overwhelmingly protective instinct she'd felt for the twins. And in all honesty the prospect of one day becoming their guardian hadn't felt remotely possible.

She realised that she hadn't really considered what this meant for her own future now. It was something she'd been good at blocking out in the last three months, after the shock of the accident and Rio's death, not to mention getting over her own injuries and caring for two highly precocious and energetic boys. It was as if she was afraid to let the enormity of it all sink in.

The solicitor looked at Cruz for a moment, and then he looked back to Trinity with something distinctly *uncomfortable* in his expression. She tensed.

'I'm not sure how aware you are of the state of Mr De Carrillo's finances when he died?'

Trinity immediately felt the scrutiny of the man to her left, as if his gaze was boring into her. His accusatory words came back to her: *'You've single-handedly run through almost every cent my brother has to his name in a bid to satisfy your greedy nature. Now you're realising Rio's fortune isn't a bottomless pit...'*

She felt breathless, as if a vice was squeezing her chest.

Until the evening of Cruz's party she hadn't been aware of any such financial difficulty. She'd only been aware that Rio was growing more and more irrational and erratic. When she'd confronted him about his behviour, they'd had a huge argument, in which the truth of exactly why he'd married her had been made very apparent. Along with his *real* agenda.

That was why Trinity had wanted to talk to Cruz—to share her concerns. However, he'd comprehensively shut that down.

She said carefully now, 'I was aware that things weren't…good. But I didn't know that it was linked to his financial situation.'

Mr. Drew looked grim. 'Well, it most probably was. The truth is that Rio was bankrupt. In these last three months the sheer extent and scale of his financial collapse has become evident, and it's comprehensive. I'm afraid that all he left behind him are debts. There is nothing to bequeath to his children. Or you.'

Trinity hadn't married Rio for his money, so this news didn't have any great impact on her. What did impact her, though, was the realisation that Cruz must have been putting money into the account that she used for day-to-day necessities for her and the boys and Mrs Jordan—the nanny Rio had hired once Trinity had married him, when her job had changed and she'd been expected to accompany him to social functions. Something she'd never felt comfortable doing…

The solicitor said, 'I'm sorry to deliver this news, Mrs De Carrillo, but even the house will have to be sold to cover his debts.'

Before she could absorb that, Cruz was standing up and saying, in a coolly authoritative tone, 'If you could leave us now, Mr. Drew, I'll go over the rest with my sister-in-law.'

The solicitor clearly had no issue with being summarily

dismissed from his own office. He gathered some papers and left, shutting the door softly behind him.

Trinity's mind was reeling, as she tried to take everything in, and revolving with a sickening sense of growing panic as to how she was going to manage caring for the boys when she didn't have a job. How could she afford to keep Mrs Jordan on?

Cruz walked over to the floor-to-ceiling windows behind the large desk, showcasing an impressive view of London's skyline.

For a long moment he said nothing, and she could only look helplessly at his broad shoulders and back. Then he turned around and a sense of déjà-vu nearly knocked her off her chair. It was so reminiscent of when she'd first met him—when she'd gone to his house in Holland Park for an interview, applying for the position of maid in his household.

She'd never met such an intimidating man in her life. Nor such a blatantly masculine man. Based on his reputation as one of the world's wealthiest bankers, she had assumed him to be older, somewhat soft... But he'd been young. And gorgeous. His tall, powerful body had looked as if it was hewn from pure granite and steel. His eyes had been disconcertingly unreadable...

'Miss Adams...did you hear my question?'

She was back in time, caught in the glare of those mesmerising eyes, his brows drawn into a frown of impatience. His Spanish accent had been barely noticeable, just the slightest intriguing inflection. She'd felt light-headed, even though she was sitting down.

'I'm sorry...what?'

Those eyes had flashed with irritation. 'I asked how old you are?'

She'd swallowed. 'I'm twenty-two. Since last week.'

Then she'd felt silly for mentioning that detail—as if

one of the richest men in the world cared when her birthday was! Not that she even knew when her birthday was for sure...

But she'd survived four rounds of intense interviews to be there to meet the man himself—evidence of how he oversaw every tiny detail of his life—so Trinity had gathered her fraying wits, drawn her shoulders back and reminded herself that she had hopes and dreams, and that if she got this job she'd be well on her way to achieving a life for herself...

'I have to hand it to you—you're as good an actress as you were three months ago when you first feigned ignorance of Rio's financial situation. But you must have known what was coming down the tracks. After all, you helped divest my brother of a small fortune.'

The past and present meshed for a moment, and then Trinity realised what Cruz had just said.

She clasped her hands tight together on her lap. 'But I didn't know.'

'Did the accident affect your memory, Trinity?' His voice held more than a note of disdain. 'Do you not recall that illuminating conversation we had before you left my house on that fateful night?'

She flushed, remembering it all too well. 'I don't have any memory of the accident, but, yes, I do recall what you said to me. You're referring to your accusation that I was responsible for Rio's financial problems.'

Cruz's mouth compressed. 'I think *ruin* would be a more accurate word.'

Trinity stood up, too agitated to stay seated. 'You're wrong. It's true that Rio spent money on me, yes, but it was for the purposes of—'

Cruz held up a hand, a distinct sneer on his face now. 'Spare me the details. I looked into Rio's accounts after he died. I know all about the personal stylist, the VIP seats to every fashion show, the haute couture dresses, private jet travel, the best hotels in the world… The list is endless. I curse the day that I hired you to work for me—because, believe me, I blame myself as much as you for ruining my brother.'

At that damning pronouncement Trinity felt something deep inside her shrivel up to protect itself. She had not been prepared for Cruz's vitriolic attack.

But then, this was the man who had wiped her taste off his mouth and looked at her with disgust when he'd realised that he'd lowered himself to the level of kissing his own maid.

Trinity bitterly recalled the intimate dinner party he'd hosted the following evening—when the gaping chasm between them had been all too apparent.

Cruz had welcomed a tall and stunningly beautiful brunette, kissing her warmly on both cheeks. As the woman had passed her fur coat to Trinity, not even glancing in her direction, Trinity had caught an expressive look from Cruz that had spoken volumes—telling her to forget what had happened. Telling her that this woman was the kind of woman he consorted with, and whatever had happened between them must be consigned to some sordid memory box, never to be taken out and examined again.

That was when she'd been unable to hold her emotions in, utterly ashamed that she'd let her crush grow to such gargantuan proportions that she'd let him actually *hurt* her. And that was when Rio, Cruz's half-brother, who had also been a guest that night, had found her outside, in a hidden corner of the garden, weeping pathetically.

He'd come outside to smoke and had sat down beside her, telling her to relax when she'd tried to rush back inside, mortified. And somehow…she still wasn't sure how… he'd managed to get her to open up, to reveal what had happened. She hadn't told him of her burgeoning feelings for

Cruz, but she probably hadn't had to. It must have been emblazoned all over her tearstained face.

'Tell me what your price is for signing away your guardianship of my nephews?'

Trinity blinked and the painful memory faded.

As she focused on his words she went cold all over. 'What did you just say?'

Cruz snapped his fingers, displeasure oozing from his tall, hard body. 'You heard me—how much will it take, Trinity, for you to get out of my nephews' lives, because I don't doubt you have a price.'

Horror curdled her insides at the thought of being removed from Mateo and Sancho. Only that morning Sancho had thrown his arms around her and said, *'I love you, Mummy...'*

She shook her head now, something much hotter replacing the horror. 'There is no price you could pay me to leave the boys.'

'I am their blood relation.'

'You've only met them a handful of times!'

Cruz snorted. 'Are you trying to tell me that you could care for them more than their own flesh and blood? You've just been using them as a meal ticket. And now that Rio's left nothing behind they're your only hope of keeping your nest feathered—presumably by extorting money out of me.'

Trinity gasped. 'I would never—'

Cruz lifted a hand. 'Spare me.'

Trinity's mouth closed as she struggled to process this. All her protective hackles were raised high now, at the suggestion that she would use her stepchildren for her own ends. She would never leave them at the mercy of a coldhearted billionaire who didn't even really know them, in spite of that flesh and blood relationship.

Impulsively she asked, 'What qualifications could you

possibly have for taking on two toddlers? Have you ever even held a baby? Changed a nappy?'

Cruz's jaw clenched. 'I do not need qualifications. I'm their uncle. I will hire the best possible staff to attend to their every need.'

His gaze narrowed on her so intently she fought against squirming under it.

'What possible qualifications could *you* have? When you came to work for me you'd left school after your A-levels with not much work experience.'

His remark went right to the heart of her and stung— badly. It stung because of the way she'd longed to impress this man at one time, and had yearned to catch his attention. It stung because of the very private dreams she'd harboured to further her education. And it stung because in all the foster homes where she'd lived through her formative years she'd instinctively found herself mothering any younger foster children, as if drawn to create what she didn't have: a family.

She pushed down the hurt at Cruz's sneering disdain now, cursing her naivety, and lifted her chin. 'I've been caring for them since they were a year old. No one is qualified to be a parent until they become one. From the moment I married Rio I became their step-parent, and I would never turn my back on them.'

'Very noble indeed. But forgive me if I don't believe you. Now, we can continue to go around in these tiresome circles, or you can just tell me how much it'll take.'

He gestured to the table and she looked down to see a chequebook.

'I will write a cheque for whatever you want, Trinity, so let's stop playing games. You've done it. Your impressive act of caring for children that aren't your own is over. You can get on with your life.'

The sheer ease with which Cruz revealed his astounding cynicism angered Trinity as much as it shocked her.

She balled her hands into fists by her sides. 'I am not playing games. And those boys are as much mine as if I'd given birth to them myself.' It hit her then—the enormity of the love she felt for them. She'd always known she loved them, but right now she'd lay her life down for them.

The thought of Cruz taking the boys and washing his hands of them the way Rio had done—abdicating all responsibility to some faceless nanny—made her feel desperate. She had to try and make him believe her.

She took a deep breath. 'Please listen to me, Cruz. The marriage wasn't what you think... The truth is that it was a marriage of convenience. The twins were primarily the reason I agreed to it. I wanted to protect them.'

Trinity could feel her heart thumping. Tension snapped between them.

Then, showing not a hint of expression, Cruz said, 'Oh, I can imagine that it was very convenient. For you. And I have no doubt that my nephews were front and centre of your machinations. I know my brother was no saint—believe me, I'm under no illusions about that. But, based on his first choice of wife, it stretches the bounds of my credulity that he would turn around and marry a mere nanny, for convenience's sake. He was a passionate man, Trinity. You are a beautiful woman. I can only imagine that you used every trick in the book to take it beyond an affair between boss and employee. After all, I have personal experience of your methods. But, believe me, the only "convenience" I see here is the way you so *conveniently* seduced your way into his bed and then into a registry office, making sure you'd be set for life.'

Trinity ignored Cruz's *'you're a beautiful woman'* because it hadn't sounded remotely complimentary. She longed to reveal that no such affair had taken place, but she felt suddenly vulnerable under that blistering gaze, all her anger draining away to be replaced with the humiliation she'd felt after that *'personal experience'* he'd spoken of.

She found the words to inform him that Rio hadn't been remotely interested in her lodging in her throat. The reality was that one brother had rejected her and another had used her for his own ends. And the fact that she was letting this get to her now was even more galling. She should be thinking of Mateo and Sancho, not her own deep insecurities.

She stood tall against the biggest threat she'd ever faced. 'I'm not going anywhere. I am their legal guardian.'

Cruz folded his arms. 'I won't hesitate to take you to court to fight for their custody if I have to. Do you really want that to happen? Who do you think the courts will favour? Their flesh-and-blood uncle, who has nothing but their best interests at heart and the means to set them up for life, or their opportunistic stepmother who systematically spent her way through her husband's wealth? Needless to say if you force this route then you will receive nothing.'

Trinity felt her blood rush south so quickly that she swayed on her feet, but she sucked in a quick breath to regain her composure before he could see it. 'You can't threaten me like this,' she said, as firmly as she could. 'I'm their legal guardian, as per Rio's wishes.'

Cruz bit out, 'I told you before—I'm not interested in playing games.'

'Neither am I!' Trinity almost wailed. 'But I'm not letting you bully me into handing over custody of Matty and Sancho.'

Cruz looked disgusted. '*Matty?* What on earth is that?'

Trinity put her hands on her hips. 'It's what Sancho has called him ever since he started talking.'

Cruz waved a hand dismissively. 'It's a ridiculous name for an heir to the De Carrillo fortune.'

Trinity went still. 'What do you mean, heir? Surely any children *you* have will be the heirs...'

Cruz was close to reaching boiling point—which wasn't helped by the fact that his libido seemed to be reaching boiling point too. He was uncomfortably aware of how Trinity's breasts pushed against the fabric of her seemingly demure silk shirt. It was buttoned to her neck, but it was the most provocative thing he'd ever seen. It made him want to push aside the desk and rip it open so he could feast his gaze on those firm swells...

Which was an unwelcome reminder of how he'd reacted that night when he'd found her in his study—*supposedly* looking for a book—testing the very limits of his control in not much more than a vest and sleep shorts, with a flimsy robe belted around her tiny waist.

It *had* broken the limits of his control, proving that he wasn't so far removed from his father after all, in spite of his best efforts.

Cruz had had her backed up against the wall of shelves, grinding his achingly hard arousal into her quivering body, his fingers buried deep in slick heat and his mouth latched around a hard nipple, before he'd come to his senses...

Cursing her silently, and reining in his thundering arousal, Cruz said, with a coolness that belied the heat under the surface, '*Mateo* and Sancho will be my heirs, as I have no intention of having any children.'

Trinity shook her head. 'Why would you say such a thing?'

Already aware that he'd said too much, Cruz clamped down on the curious urge to explain that as soon as he'd heard Rio was having children he'd felt a weight lift off his shoulders, not having been really aware until then that he'd never relished the burden of producing an heir for the sake of the family business.

He'd learnt from a young age what it was to have to stand by helplessly and watch his own half-brother being treated as nothing just because he was the result of an affair. He'd experienced the way parents—the people who were meant to love you the most—sometimes had scant regard for their offspring. Cruz might have been the privileged legitimate heir, but he'd been treated more like an employee than a loved son.

He'd never felt that he had the necessary skills to be a father, and he'd never felt a desire to test that assertion. However, his nephews had changed things. And the fact that Rio was no longer alive *really* changed things now. And the fact that this woman believed she could control their fate was abominable.

Cruz was aware that he barely knew his nephews—every time he saw them they hid behind Trinity's legs, or their nanny's skirts. And until Rio had died he hadn't felt any great desire to connect with them...not knowing *how* to, in all honesty. But now an overwhelming instinct to protect them rose up in him and surprised him with its force. It reminded him of when he'd felt so protective of Rio when he'd been much smaller, and the reminder was poignant. And pertinent. He hadn't been able to protect Rio, but he could protect his nephews.

Perhaps Trinity thought she'd get more out of him like this. He rued the day she'd ever appeared in his life.

Curtly he said, 'I'll give you tonight to think it over. Tomorrow, midday, I'll come to the house—and trust me when I say that if you don't have your price ready by then, you'll have to prepare yourself for a legal battle after which you'll wish that you'd taken what I'm offering.'

CHAPTER TWO

ON THE BUS back to Rio's house near Regent's Park—
Trinity had never considered it hers—she was still reeling.
She felt as if someone had physically punched her. Cruz
had...except without using fists...and the reminder that
she'd once fancied herself almost in love with him was
utterly mortifying now.

The full enormity of his distrust in her was shocking—
as was his threat that he would take her to court to get the
boys if he had to.

She didn't need Cruz to tell her that she wouldn't fare
well up against one of the world's wealthiest and most
powerful men. As soon as his lawyers looked into her
background and saw that she'd grown up in foster homes,
with no family stability to her name, she'd be out of Matty
and Sancho's lives.

It didn't even occur to her to consider Cruz's offer—
the thought of leaving the twins in his cold and autocratic
care was anathema to her.

Being in such close proximity to him again had left her
feeling on edge and jittery. Too aware of her body. Sometimes the memory of that cataclysmic night in Cruz's study
came back like a taunt. And, no matter how much she tried
to resist it, it was too powerful for her to push down. It
was as vivid as if it had just happened. The scene of her
spectacular humiliation.

The fact that Cruz obviously hated himself for what had
happened was like the lash of a whip every time she saw
him. As if she needed to be reminded of his disgust! As
if he needed another reason to hate her now! Because that

much was crystal-clear. He'd judged her and condemned her—he hadn't even wanted to hear her defence.

Trinity tried to resist thinking about the past, but the rain beating relentlessly against the bus windows didn't help. She felt as if she was in a cocoon...

She'd been working as Cruz's housemaid for approximately six months, and one night, unable to sleep, she'd gone down to the study to find a new book. Cruz had told her to feel welcome to read his books after he'd found her curled up in a chair reading one day.

Trinity had been very aware that she was developing a monumentally pathetic crush on her enigmatic boss—she'd even read about him in one of his discarded copies of the *Financial Times*.

She'd loved to read the papers, even though she hadn't understood half of what they talked about, and it had been her ambition to understand it all some day. She'd finally felt as if she was breaking away from her past, and that she could possibly prove that she didn't have to be limited by the fact that her own parents had abandoned her.

Cruz had epitomised success and keen intelligence, and Trinity had been helplessly impressed and inspired. Needless to say he was the kind of man who would never notice someone like her in a million years, no matter how polite to her he was. Except sometimes she'd look up and find him watching her with a curious expression on his face, and it would make her feel hot and flustered. Self-conscious...

When she'd entered the study that night, she'd done so cautiously, even though she'd known Cruz was out at a function. She'd turned on a dim light and gone straight to the bookshelves, and had spent a happy few minutes looking for something to read among the very broad range he had. She'd been intrigued by the fact that alongside serious tomes on economics there were battered copies of John Le Carré and Agatha Christie. They humanised a very intimidating man.

She'd almost jumped out of her skin when a deep voice had said, with a touch of humour, 'Good to know it's not a burglar rifling through my desk.'

Trinity had immediately dropped the book she was looking at and turned to see Cruz in the doorway, breathtakingly gorgeous in a classic tuxedo, his bow tie rakishly undone. And her brain had just…melted.

Eventually, when her wits had returned, she'd bent down to pick up the book, acutely aware of her state of undress, and started gabbling. 'I'm sorry… I just wanted to get a book…couldn't sleep…'

She'd held the book in front of her like a shield. As if it might hide her braless breasts, covered only by the flimsiest material. But something in Cruz's lazy stance changed as his eyes had raked over her, and the air had suddenly been charged. Electric.

Her eyes had widened as he'd closed the distance between them. She'd been mesmerised. Glued to the spot. Glued to his face as it was revealed in the shadows of the room, all stark lines and angles. He'd taken the book she was holding out of her hand and looked at it, before putting it back on the shelf. He'd been so close she'd been able to smell his scent, and had wanted to close her eyes to breathe it in even deeper. She'd felt dizzy.

Then he'd reached out and touched her hair, taking a strand between two fingers and letting it run between them. The fact that he'd come so close…was touching her…had been so unlikely that she hadn't been able to move.

Her lower body had tightened with a kind of need she'd never felt before. She'd cursed her inexperience in that moment—cursed the fact that living in foster homes all her life had made her put up high walls of defence because she'd never been settled anywhere long enough to forge any kind of meaningful relationship.

She'd known she should have moved...that this was ridiculous. That the longer she stood there, in thrall to her gorgeous boss, the sooner he'd step back and she'd be totally exposed. She'd never let anyone affect her like this before, but somehow, without even trying, he'd just slipped under her skin...

But then he'd looked at her with a molten light in his eyes and said, 'I want you, Trinity Adams. I know I shouldn't, but I do.'

He'd let her hair go.

His words had shocked her so much that even though she'd known that was the moment to turn and walk out, her bare feet had stayed glued to the floor.

A reckless desire had rushed through her, heady and dangerous, borne out of the impossible reality that Cruz De Carrillo was looking at her like this...saying he wanted her. She was a nobody. She came from nothing. And yet at that moment she'd felt seen in a way she'd never experienced before.

It had come out of her, unbidden, from the deepest part of her. One word. *'Please...'*

Cruz had looked at her for a long moment, and then he'd muttered something in Spanish as he'd taken her arms in his hands and walked her backwards until she'd hit the bookshelves with a soft *thunk*.

And then he'd kissed her.

But it had been more like a beautifully brutal awakening than a kiss. She'd gone on fire in seconds, and discovered that she was capable of sudden voracious desires and needs.

His kiss had drugged her, taking her deep into herself

and a world of new and amazing sensations. The feel of his rough tongue stroking hers had been so intimate and wicked, and yet more addictive than anything she'd ever known. She'd understood it in that moment—what the power of a drug might be.

Then his big hands had touched her waist, belly, breasts, cupping their full weight. They'd been a little rough, unsteady, and she hadn't expected that of someone who was always so cool. In control.

The thought that she might be doing this to him had been unbelievable.

He'd pulled open her robe so that he could pull down her vest top and take her nipple into his mouth, making Trinity moan and writhe like a wanton under his hands. She remembered panting, opening her legs, sighing with ecstasy when he'd found the naked moist heat of her body and touched her there, rubbing back and forth, exploring with his fingers, making her gasp and twist higher and higher in an inexorable climb as he'd spoken low Spanish words into her ear until she'd broken apart, into a million shards of pleasure so intense that she'd felt emotion leak out of her eyes.

And that was when a cold breeze had skated over her skin. Some foreboding. Cruz had pulled back, but he'd still had one hand between her legs and the other on her bared breast. He'd been breathing as harshly as her, and they'd looked at each other for a long moment.

He'd blinked, as if waking from the sensual spell that had come over them, and at the same time he'd taken his hands off her and said, 'What the hell…?'

He'd stepped away from her so fast she'd lurched forward and had to steady herself, acutely aware of her clothes in disarray. She'd pulled her robe around herself with shaking hands.

Cruz had wiped the back of his hand across his mouth

and Trinity had wanted to disappear—to curl up in a ball and hide away from the dawning realisation and horror on his face.

'I'm sorry... I—' Her voice had felt scratchy. She hadn't even been sure why she was apologising.

He'd cut her off. '*No*. This was *my* fault. It should never have happened.'

He'd turned icy and distant so quickly that if her body hadn't still been throbbing with the after-effects of her first orgasm she might have doubted it had even happened— that he'd lost his control for a brief moment and shown her the fire burning under that cool surface.

'It was an unforgivable breach of trust.'

Miserable, Trinity had said, 'It was my fault too.'

He'd said nothing, and then, slightly accusingly, 'Do you usually walk around the house dressed like that?'

Trinity had gone cold again. 'What exactly are you saying?'

Cruz had dragged his gaze back up. His cheeks had been flushed, hair a little mussed. She'd never seen anyone sexier or more undone and not happy about it.

'Nothing,' he'd bitten out. 'Just...get out of here and forget this ever happened. It was completely inappropriate. I *never* mix business with pleasure, and I'm not about to start.' He'd looked away from her, a muscle pulsing in his jaw.

Right then Trinity had never felt so cheap in her life. He obviously couldn't bear to look at her a moment longer. She'd felt herself closing inwards, aghast that she'd let herself fall into a dream of feeling special so easily. She should have known better. Cruz De Carrillo took beautiful, sophisticated and intelligent women to his bed. He didn't have sordid fumbles with staff in his library.

The divide between them had yawned open like a huge dark chasm. Her naivety had slapped her across the face.

Without saying another word, she'd fled from the room.

Trinity forcibly pushed the memory back down deep, where it belonged. Her stop came into view and she got up and waited for the bus to come to a halt.

As she walked back to the huge and ostentatious house by Regent's Park she spied Mrs Jordan in the distance with the double buggy.

Her heart lifted and she half ran, half walked to meet them. The boys jumped up and down in their seats with arms outstretched when they spotted her. She hugged each of them close, revelling in their unique babyish smell, which was already changing as they grew more quickly than she knew how to keep up with them.

Something fierce gripped her inside as she held them tight. She was the only mother they'd ever really known, and she would not abandon them for anything.

When she stood up, Mrs Jordan looked at her with concern. 'Are you all right, dear? You look very pale.'

Trinity forced a brittle smile. She couldn't really answer—because what could she say? That Cruz was going to come the next day and turn their world upside down? That lovely Mrs Jordan might be out of a job? That Trinity would be consigned to a scrap heap somewhere?

The boys would be upset and bewildered, facing a whole new world...

A sob made its way up her throat, but she forced it down and said the only thing she could. 'We need to talk.'

The following day, at midday on the dot, the doorbell rang. Trinity looked nervously at Mrs Jordan, who was as pale as she had been yesterday. They each held a twin in their arms, and Matty and Sancho were unusually quiet, as if sensing the tension in the air. Trinity had hated worrying the older woman, but it wouldn't have been fair not to warn her about what Cruz had said...

Mrs Jordan went to open the door, and even though Trinity had steeled herself she still wasn't prepared to see Cruz's broad, tall frame filling the doorway, a sleek black chauffeur-driven car just visible in the background. He wore a three-piece suit and an overcoat against the English spring chill. He looked vital and intimidating and gorgeous.

He stepped inside and the boys curled into Trinity and Mrs Jordan. They were always shy around their uncle, whom Matty called *'the big man'*.

'Mr De Carrillo, how nice to see you,' Mrs Jordan said, ever the diplomat.

Cruz looked away from Trinity to the older woman. There was only the slightest softening on his face. 'You too, Mrs Jordan.'

They exchanged pleasantries, and Mrs Jordan asked if he wanted tea or coffee before bustling off to the kitchen with Sancho. Trinity noticed that he'd looked at his nephews warily.

Then he looked at her with narrowed eyes. 'I presume we can talk alone?'

She wanted to say no, and run with the boys and Mrs Jordan somewhere safe. But she couldn't.

She nodded jerkily and said, 'Just let me get the boys set up for lunch and then I'll be with you.'

Cruz just inclined his head slightly, but he said *sotto voce*, as she passed him to follow Mrs Jordan to the kitchen, 'Don't make me wait, Trinity.'

Once they were out of earshot, Matty said in an awe-struck voice. 'Tha's the big man!'

Trinity replied as butterflies jumped around her belly. 'Yes, sweetie. He's your uncle, remember…?'

'Unk-*el*…' Matty repeated carefully, as if testing out the word.

Trinity delayed as much as she dared, making sure the

boys were strapped securely into their high chairs, but then she had to leave.

Mrs Jordan handed her a tray containing the tea and coffee, and looked at her expressively. 'I'm sure he'll do what's right for the boys and you, dear. Don't worry.'

Trinity felt shame curl through her as she walked to the drawing room with the tray. She'd been too cowardly to tell Mrs Jordan the truth of Cruz's opinion of her. The woman believed that he only wanted custody of his nephews because he was their last remaining blood relative.

Stopping at the door for a second, she took a breath and wondered if she should have worn something smarter than jeans and a plain long-sleeved jumper. But it was too late. She balanced the tray on her raised knee, then opened the door and went in. Her heart thumped as she saw Cruz, with his overcoat off, standing at the main window that looked out over the opulent gardens at the back of the house.

She avoided looking at him and went over to where a low table sat between two couches. She put the tray down and glanced up. 'Coffee, wasn't it?'

Cruz came and sat down on the couch opposite hers. 'Yes.'

No *please*. No niceties.

Trinity was very aware of how the fabric of his trousers pulled taut over his powerful thighs. She handed over the coffee in a cup, grateful that this time her hands were fairly steady. She sipped at her own tea, as if that might fortify her, and wished it was something slightly stronger.

After a strained moment Trinity knew she couldn't avoid him for ever. She looked at him and blurted out, 'Why are you doing this now? If you're so sure I'm... what you say I am...why didn't you just step in after Rio's death?'

Cruz took a lazy sip of his coffee and put the cup down,

for all the world as if this was a cordial visit. He looked at her. 'I, unlike you, grieved my brother's death—'

'That's not fair,' Trinity breathed.

Okay, so Rio had made her angry—especially at the end—and theirs hadn't been a real marriage, but she had felt a certain kinship with him. They hadn't been so different, as he'd told her—both abandoned by their parents. But then he'd betrayed her trust and her loyalty.

Cruz continued as if she'd said nothing. 'Once the state of Rio's finances became apparent, there was a lot of fire-fighting to be done. Deals he'd been involved in had to be tied up. I had to search for his mother to let her know what had happened—'

'Did you find her?' Trinity's heart squeezed as she thought of the impossible dream she never let herself indulge in: that some day she'd find *her* mother.

Cruz shook his head. 'No—and yes. She died some years ago, of a drug overdose.'

'Oh,' she said, feeling sad.

'I knew when the reading of the will would be taking place, and I wanted to see your face when you realised that there was nothing for you. And I'd been keeping an eye on you, so I knew what you were up to and how my nephews were.'

Trinity gasped. 'You had us followed?'

Cruz shrugged minutely. 'I couldn't be sure you wouldn't try to disappear. And you're the very public widow of a man most people still believe was a millionaire, with two small vulnerable children in your care. It was for your protection as much as my surveillance.'

Before she could fully absorb that, he went on, with palpable impatience.

'Look, I really don't have time for small talk, Trinity. Tell me how much you want so that I can get on with making the necessary arrangements to have my custody of my nephews legalised.'

His words were like a red rag to a bull—having it confirmed that he'd just been biding his time. That she'd never really registered on his radar as anyone worth giving the benefit of the doubt to.

She put her cup down with a clatter on the tray and glared at him. 'How dare you? Do you really think it's that simple? They are not pawns, Cruz. They are two small human beings who depend on structure and routine, who have lost both their parents at a very vulnerable age. Mrs Jordan and I are the most consistent people in their lives and you want to rip them away from that?'

She stood up then, too agitated to keep sitting down. Cruz stood too, and Trinity immediately felt intimidated.

He bit out, 'I want to take them away from a malignant influence. *You.* Are you seriously telling me you're prepared to go up against me? You know what'll happen if you do. You'll lose.'

'No!' Trinity cried passionately. 'The twins will lose. Do you know they've only just stopped asking for their *papa* every night? Because that's usually when he came to see them, to say goodnight. Their world has been turned upside down and you want to do it again. Who will be their primary carer? Don't tell me it's going to be *you.*' Trinity would never normally be so blunt or so cruel, but she felt desperate. 'Have you noticed how they look at you? They're intimidated by you. They hardly know who you are.'

Clearly unaccustomed to having anyone speak to him like this, Cruz flashed his eyes in disapproval. 'If anyone has been these boys' primary carer, I'd wager it's been Mrs Jordan. There's no reason why she can't remain as their nanny. But you have no claim on these boys beyond the legal guardianship you seduced out of Rio in a bid to protect your own future.'

Trinity's hands balled into fists. Her nails cut into her palms but she barely noticed. She wondered how she'd ever felt remotely tender about this man. 'That is *not* true. I love these boys as if they were my own.'

Cruz let out a curt laugh. 'I *know* that's not true.'

His smile faded, and his face became sterner than she'd ever seen it.

'And do you know why? Because Rio and I both learned that the people who are meant to love you the most *don't*. There's no such thing as an unbreakable bond.'

The fire left Trinity's belly. She felt shaky after the rush of adrenalin. Rio had told her about the way he'd been treated like an unwelcome guest in his own father's home. How his mother had abandoned him. It had played on all her sympathies. Now she wondered about Cruz's experience, and hated herself for this evidence that he still got to her.

'Not all parents were like yours or Rio's.'

Cruz arched a brow. 'And you know this from personal experience, when you grew up in a series of foster homes? Your experience wasn't too far removed from ours, was it, Trinity? So tell me how you know something I don't.'

Trinity went very still. 'How do you know that?'

He watched her assessingly. 'I run background checks on all my staff.' His lip curled. 'To think I actually felt some admiration for you—abandoned by your parents, brought up in care, but clearly ambitious and determined to make something of yourself. I seriously underestimated how little you were actually prepared to work to that end.'

The unfairness of his assessment winded her when she thought of the back-breaking work she'd done, first as a chambermaid in a hotel, then as a maid in his house, before becoming nanny to two demanding babies. And then Rio's *wife*.

Feeling seriously vulnerable upon finding out that Cruz

had known about her past all this time and had mentioned it so casually, she said, 'My experience has nothing to do with this.'

Liar, said a voice. It did, but not in the way Cruz believed.

'I love Matty and Sancho and I will do anything to protect them.'

Cruz was like an immovable force. 'You have some nerve to mention love. Are you seriously trying to tell me you loved Rio?'

Feeling desperate, she said, 'I told you—it wasn't like that.'

He glared at her. 'No, it wasn't. At least you're being honest about that.'

Trinity shivered under his look. His anger was palpable now. She said then, 'I did care for him.'

Before Cruz could respond to that there was a commotion outside, and Mrs Jordan appeared in the doorway with a wailing Sancho, who was leaning out of her arms towards Trinity, saying pitifully, *'Mummy...'*

Everything suddenly forgotten, she rushed forward and took him into her arms, rubbing his back and soothing him.

Mrs Jordan said apologetically, 'Matty hit him over the head with his plastic cup. It's nothing serious, but he's fractious after not sleeping well again last night.'

Trinity nodded and Mrs Jordan left to go back to Matty. She was walking up and down, soothing a now hiccupping Sancho, when she realised Cruz was staring at her with an angry look on his face.

He said almost accusingly, 'What's wrong with him?'

Suddenly Trinity was incredibly weary. 'Nothing much. He had a bug and he hasn't been sleeping, so he's in bad form. Matty just wound him up.' When Cruz didn't look appeased she said, 'Really, it's nothing.' She felt exposed under Cruz's judgemental look. 'Let me settle him down for a nap. That's all he needs.'

* * *

Cruz watched Trinity walk out of the room with Sancho in her arms, his nephew's small, chubby ones wrapped tight around her neck, his flushed face buried in her neck as if it was a habitual reflex for seeking comfort. He had stopped crying almost as soon as he'd gone into her arms.

Cruz had felt a totally uncharacteristic sense of helplessness seeing his nephew like that. It reminded him uncomfortably of his own childhood, hearing Rio cry but being unable to do anything to help him—either because Rio would glare at him with simmering resentment or his father would hold him back with a cruel hand.

Sancho's cries hadn't fazed Trinity, though. In fact she'd looked remarkably capable.

Feeling angry all over again, and this time for a reason he couldn't really pinpoint, Cruz turned back to the window. He ran a hand through his hair and then loosened his tie, feeling constricted. And he felt even more constricted in another area of his anatomy when he recalled how his gaze had immediately dropped to take in the provocative swell of Trinity's bottom as she'd walked away, her long legs encased in those faded jeans that clung like a second skin.

Damn her.

Witnessing this little incident was forcing Cruz to stop and think about what he was doing here. It was obvious that not only had Trinity seduced Rio for her own ends, she'd also ensured that the boys would depend on her...in case of this very scenario?

Cruz thought of pursuing his plans to take Trinity to court to fight her for custody, but he'd already seen what a good actress she was. If someone were to come to the house and see her interacting with his nephews they wouldn't be able to help being swayed by her *apparent* love and concern. As he had just been.

And did he really want to court a PR frenzy by pitting himself against the grieving widow of his brother? He knew she wasn't grieving—she wasn't even pretending. But no one else would see that. They'd only see him, a ruthless billionaire, protecting his family fortune.

It had taken him since his father's death to change the perception his father had left behind of a failing and archaic bank, blighted by his father's numerous high-profile affairs. Did he really want to jeopardise all that hard work?

Something hardened inside him as he had to acknowledge how neatly Trinity had protected herself. She was potentially even worse than he'd thought—using his nephews like this, manipulating them to need her.

She'd lived a quiet life since Rio's death—she'd only moved between the house, the local shops and the nearby park. No shopping on Bond Street or high-profile social events.

When she'd been with Rio, Cruz had seen countless pictures of them at parties and premieres, so she had to be approaching the end of her boredom threshold.

He thought again of her assertion that she loved the boys... He couldn't countenance for a second that she loved these children who weren't even her own flesh and blood.

A memory of his own mother came back with startling clarity—he'd been a young teenager and he'd confronted her one day, incensed on her behalf that his father had been photographed in the papers with his latest mistress.

She'd just looked at him and said witheringly, 'The only mistake he made, Cruz, was getting caught. This is how our world works.' She'd laughed then—nastily. '*Dios mio*, please tell me you're not so naive as to believe we married because we actually had *feelings* for one another?'

He'd looked at his mother in shock. No, he'd never laboured under the misapprehension that any such thing as *affection* existed between his parents, but he'd realised in that moment that some tiny part of him that hadn't been obliterated after years of only the most perfunctory parenting had still harboured a kernel of hope that something meaningful existed... Shame had engulfed him for being so naive.

She'd said then, with evident bitterness, 'I was all but packaged up and sent to your father, because our two families belong to great dynasties and it was a strategic match. I did my duty and bore him a son, and I put up with his bastard son living under this very roof, and his mistresses— because, no matter what he does, this family's legacy is safe with you, and *I* have ensured that. That is all that matters in this life Cruz. Cultivating our great name and protecting it. One of these days your father will die, and as far as I'm concerned it can't come soon enough. Because then *you* will restore this family's reputation and fortune. That is your duty and your destiny, above all else.'

She'd died not long after that speech. The memory of her had faded but her words hadn't. *Duty and destiny.* There was no room for emotion, and he'd had to acknowledge the enormity of what he stood to inherit. He'd become a man that day, in more ways than one, leaving behind any childish vulnerabilities and misconceptions.

And because he'd stepped up to that responsibility he now had something solid to pass on to his nephews. They aroused something in him that he'd only felt before for Rio—an urge to protect and forge a bond. He'd become Rio's guardian while he'd still been underage, and he wanted to do the same for his vulnerable nephews. He vowed now that they would not go the way of their father. By the time they came of age they would know how to handle their legacy...he would make sure of it.

When Cruz had realised that he hadn't been named as guardian after Rio's death he'd felt inexplicably hurt, even though he'd known that he was hardly in a position to take on two small children he barely knew. It had been like a slap from beyond the grave, and he'd had to wonder if the rapprochement he'd believed to be present in his relationship with Rio had actually been real.

Or, as he'd come to suspect, was it more likely to have been someone else's influence?

Cruz had looked at Trinity, dressed in black on the other side of Rio's grave at the funeral, as his brother had been lowered into the ground. Her face had been covered in a gauzy veil, her body encased in a snug-fitting black suit. And that was when he'd vowed to do whatever it took to make sure her influence over his nephews was thwarted. He wanted them under his protection—away from a gold-digging manipulator.

Suddenly an audacious idea occurred to him. He immediately thrust it aside—appalled that he'd even thought it. But it wouldn't go away. It took root, and as he looked at it analytically it held a kind of horrific appeal.

He stared out over the gardens without really seeing them, and finally had to acknowledge grimly that there was really only one option where Trinity was concerned—but was he prepared to go to those lengths?

His gut answered him. *Yes.*

As if fate was contriving to make sure he didn't have time to change his mind he heard a noise and turned around to see Trinity coming back into the room. Her hair was pulled back into a low ponytail, but loose tendrils curled around her face. He noticed for the first time that there were delicate smudges of colour under her cornflower-blue eyes. Evidence of fatigue.

He ruthlessly pushed down a very curious sensation he'd never felt in relation to a woman before—and certainly not one he welcomed for this one: *concern.*

He faced her and saw how she tensed as she came towards him, folding her arms in a defensive gesture. Her chin tilting towards him mutinously.

With not a little relish, Cruz said, 'I have a solution which I think will work for both of us, my nephews and Mrs Jordan.'

He could see Trinity's arms tighten fractionally over her chest and he focused on her treacherously beautiful face. Even now she looked as innocent as the naive twenty-two-year-old who had come to work for him. Except, of course, she hadn't been naive. Or innocent. And she was about to face the repercussions of her actions.

'What solution?'

Cruz waited a beat and then said, very deliberately, 'Marriage, Trinity. You're going to marry me.'

CHAPTER THREE

For a moment all Trinity heard was a roaring in her ears. She shook her head but Cruz was still looking at her with that expression on his face. Determined.

She asked weakly, 'Did you just say marriage?'

'Yes, I did.'

Trinity's arms were so tight across her chest she was almost cutting off her air supply. 'That is the most ridiculous thing I've ever heard.' And yet why was there an illicit shiver deep in her belly at the thought of being married to this man?

Cruz started to stroll towards her and Trinity had a very keen sense that he was a predator, closing in on his prey.

'Even though I know I'd win in a courtroom battle for the twins, I don't really have the inclination to invite unnecessarily adverse PR in my direction by pitting myself against my brother's widow. And from what I've seen it's evident to me that Mateo and Sancho are clearly attached to you.'

'Of course they are,' she said shakily. 'I'm all they've known as a mother since they were one.'

He stopped within touching distance and Trinity's breath hitched at his sheer charisma. She forced herself to fill her lungs. She couldn't afford to let him distract her.

'Why on earth would you suggest marriage?'

He grimaced, 'You are legally my nephews' guardian, and I don't trust you not to exert your right to do something drastic. Marriage will make me their legal guardian too, and I'm not prepared to settle for anything less to ensure their protection.'

Trinity shook her head and took a step back, hating

herself for it but needing some space. 'You're crazy if you think I'll agree.'

With lethal softness he said now, 'Who do you think has been funding your existence these past few months?'

'You,' she said miserably.

'If you were to walk out of this house with my two nephews that allowance would be stopped immediately. How on earth do you think you would cope without a nanny?'

Desperation clawed upwards. 'I could get a job.'

Cruz was scathing. 'You'd be happy to lower yourself to Mrs Jordan's status again? Because that's all you're qualified for—either working as a maid or as a nanny.'

Trinity refused to let him intimidate her. 'Of course— if I had to.' A voice screamed at her—how on earth could she work with two small children in tow?

Cruz was obdurate, and Trinity knew with a sinking feeling that one way or the other he wasn't leaving until he'd got what he wanted. Her. And his nephews.

'It's very simple. I don't trust you not to take advantage of your position. And you seem to be forgetting a very pertinent fact.' He looked at her.

Eventually, with extreme reluctance and the sensation of a net closing around her, she said, 'What fact?'

'Since Rio's death those boys have had nothing but their name. The only way they will receive their inheritance now is through me, and I'm not going to let that happen unless you marry me.'

The net closed around Trinity as the full significance of that sank in. She would be responsible for not letting Matty and Sancho receive their inheritance?

'That's blackmail,' she breathed, astounded at his ruthlessness.

Cruz all but shrugged, supremely unperturbed. 'Their legacy is considerable, and as such I have a responsibility to see that it, and they, are protected.'

Affront coursed through her. 'I would never touch what's theirs.'

Cruz's lip curled. 'And yet you managed to divest Rio of a small fortune within less than a year of marriage?'

Trinity opened her mouth to defend herself again but from the look on Cruz's face she knew it would be pointless to say anything. Not in this emotive atmosphere.

She whirled away from that mocking look in his eyes and took refuge by a solid object—the couch. When she felt relatively composed again, she turned back to face him.

'There has to be some other way.' She seized on an idea. 'I can sign something. A contract that says I have no claim to their inheritance.'

Cruz shook his head and moved, coming closer. 'No. Marriage is the only option I'm prepared to consider. I've decided to move back to the De Carrillo ancestral home in Spain, near Seville. The bank is flourishing here in the UK, and in America. Its reputation has been restored. It's time to build on that, and presenting a united family front will only strengthen the business and in turn my nephews' legacy.'

Rendered speechless, Trinity could only listen as Cruz went on.

'Locking you into a marriage with me is the only way they'll get their inheritance and I'll be satisfied that you're not going to prove to be a threat to my nephews. And as it happens a convenient wife will suit my needs very well. But I'm afraid I can't offer you the bling of married life with Rio. You might have been keeping a low profile since my brother died, but I would estimate that once the reality of living in a remote *castillo* hits you'll be climbing the walls and looking for a divorce before the year is out...which I'll be only too happy to grant once I've got full custody of my nephews.'

The extent of his cynicism shocked her anew. She'd

surmised from Rio's account of his early life that things probably hadn't been idyllic for Cruz either, but she'd never imagined that he carried such a deep-rooted seam of distrust.

Trinity hated it that it aroused her empathy and curiosity—again. She cursed herself. She'd felt empathy for Rio and she'd let him manipulate her. If it hadn't been for Mateo and Sancho she'd tell Cruz where to shove his autocratic orders and storm out.

But how could she? He was threatening to withhold their very legacy if she didn't comply. And there was no way she was leaving her boys in his cold and cynical care alone. She was all they had now.

Surely, she thought quickly, if she said yes he'd realise what he was doing—marrying someone he hated himself for kissing—and agree to make some kind of compromise? Trinity shoved down the betraying hurt that Cruz would never even be suggesting such a thing if she didn't have something he wanted. His nephews.

She called his bluff. 'You leave me no choice. Yes, I'll marry you.'

She waited for Cruz to blanch, or for realisation to hit and for him to tell her that he'd only been testing her commitment, but he showed no emotion. Nor triumph. After a beat he just looked at his watch, and then back at her, as cold as ice.

'Good. I'll have my team draw up a pre-nuptial agreement and organise a fast and discreet civil wedding within the next few weeks, after which we'll leave directly for Spain.'

He had turned and was walking out of the room before the shock reverberating through Trinity subsided enough for her to scramble after him—clearly he was not a man who was easily bluffed. He was deadly serious about this.

His hand was on the doorknob when she came to a

stumbling halt behind him, breathless. 'Wait a minute—you don't really want to marry me. What about falling in love?'

Cruz turned around with an incredulous look on his face, and then threw his head back and laughed so abruptly that Trinity flinched. When he looked at her again his eyes glittered like dark golden sapphires.

'*Love?* Now you really are over-acting. Choice in marriage and falling in love are best left to the deluded. Look where infatuation got my brother—driven to fatal destruction. I have no time for such emotions or weaknesses. This marriage will be one in name only, purely to protect my nephews from your grasping hands, and you will fulfil your role as my wife to the best of your ability.'

Trinity tried one more time. 'You don't have to do this. I would never harm my stepsons, or take their inheritance from them.'

Cruz's eyes gleamed with stark intent. 'I don't believe you, and I don't trust you. So, yes, we *are* doing this. You'll need to see if Mrs Jordan is happy to stay in my employment and come to Spain. If not, we'll have to hire another nanny. The sooner you come to terms with this new reality and start preparing the boys for the move the easier it will be for me to make the necessary arrangements.'

For long minutes after he'd walked out Trinity stood there in shock. What had she just done?

True to his word, just over two weeks later Trinity stood beside Cruz De Carrillo in a register office. He was dressed in a sleek dark grey suit, white shirt and matching tie. She wore an understated cream silk knee-length sheath dress with matching jacket. Her hair was up in a smooth chignon, her make-up light.

In the end resistance had been futile. No matter which way she'd looked at it, she'd kept coming back to the fact that she wasn't prepared to walk away from Mateo and Sancho after all they'd been through—as well as the fact that the thought of leaving them made her feel as if someone was carving her heart out of her chest.

By agreeing to marry Rio she'd at least felt that she could offer them some permanence, which she'd never had. She hadn't wanted them to go through the same insecurity…and now she was in exactly the same position. So it had come down to this: she had nowhere to go, and no one to turn to.

When she'd put Cruz's plan to Mrs Jordan, the woman had thought about it, consulted with her son who was at university in Scotland, and then agreed to stay with them as long as she could be guaranteed regular visits home. Trinity had felt emotional, knowing that at least she'd have Mrs Jordan's quiet and calm support.

She was acutely conscious now of Cruz's tall, hard body beside her as the registrar spoke the closing words of the ceremony. She was all but a prisoner to this man now. The perfect chattel. She looked at the simple gold band on her finger that marked her as married for the second time in her life. This time, though, she thought a little hysterically, at least she wasn't remotely deluded about her husband's intentions.

'I now pronounce you husband and wife. Congratulations. You may kiss your wife, Mr De Carrillo.'

Slowly, reluctantly, Trinity turned to face Cruz. She looked up. Even though she wore high heels, he still towered over her.

Cruz just looked at her for a long moment. Trinity's breath was trapped in her throat like a bird. Was he going to humiliate her in front of their small crowd of witnesses—largely made up of his legal team—by refusing to kiss her?

But then, just when she expected him to turn away

dismissively, he lowered his head and his mouth touched hers. Firm. Cool. His lips weren't tightly shut, and neither were hers, so for a second their breaths mingled, and in that moment a flame of pure heat licked through her with such force that she was hurled back in time to that incendiary kiss in his study.

Before she could control her reaction, though, Cruz was pulling back to look down at her again with those hard, glittering eyes. They transmitted a silent but unmistakable message: he would do the bare minimum in public to promote an image of unity, but that was as far as it would go.

Trinity was humiliated by her reaction, by the fact that he still had such a devastating effect on her. And terrified at the prospect of him realising it. She tried to pull her hand free of his but he only tightened his grip, reminding her of how trapped she was.

She glared up at him.

'Smile for the photos, *querida*.'

Trinity followed Cruz's look to see a photographer waiting. Of course. This was all part of his plan, wasn't it? To send out a message of a family united.

Aware that she must look more like someone about to be tipped over the edge of a plank than a besotted bride, Trinity forced a smile and flinched only slightly when the flash went off.

Cruz could hear his nephews chattering happily as they were fed at the back of the plane. Then he heard softer, lower tones… Trinity's… He tensed. Any sense of satisfaction at the fact that he'd achieved what he'd set out to achieve was gone. He cursed silently. Who was he kidding? He'd been tense since he'd left her standing in that room in Rio's house, with her eyes like two huge pools of blue, and a face leached of all colour.

It should have given him an immense sense of accomplishment to know he'd pulled the rug from under her feet, but he'd walked away that day with far more complicated emotions in his gut—and a very unwelcome reminder of when he'd seen a similar look of stunned shock on her face...the night he'd kissed her.

She'd been the last person he'd expected to see when he'd walked into his study that night, weary from a round of engaging in mind-numbingly boring small-talk. And fending off women who, up until a few months before, would have tempted him. His mind had been full of...*her*. And then to find her there, stretching up, long legs bare and exposed, the lush curve of her bottom visible under the short robe and the even more provocative curve of her unbound breasts... It was as if she'd walked straight out of his deepest fantasy...

He could still recall the second he'd come to his senses, when he'd realised he was moments away from lifting her up against his shelves and finding explosive release in her willing body, all soft and hot and *wet*. No other woman had ever caused him to lose it like that. But she'd been his *employee*. Someone he'd been in a position of power over.

The stark realisation that he was following in his father's footsteps in spite of every effort he'd made to remove the shadow of that man's reputation had been sickening. He was no better after all.

He'd been harsh afterwards...angry at his reaction... demanding to know what she was doing there as if it had been her fault. He'd felt like a boor. Little had he known then that she'd obviously been waiting until he got home and had made sure he found her...

It was galling. A sign of weakness. Cruz scowled. Trinity had no power over his emotions. She represented a very fleeting moment in time when he'd forgotten who he was.

The reality of his situation hit him then—in marrying Trinity he was consigning himself to a life with a woman he would never trust. But the sacrifice would be worth it for his nephews' sake.

At least now she was under his control and his watchful eye.

He'd felt anything *but* watchful earlier, though, when she'd turned to face him in that sterile register office and everyone had waited for their kiss. He'd had no intention of kissing her—it would show her how it would be between them. And prove that he could control himself around her... But for a split second his gaze had dropped to that lush mouth and every cool, logical intention had scattered, to be replaced with an all too familiar desire just to take one sip, one taste...

So he'd bent his head, seeing the flash of surprise in her eyes, and touched his mouth to hers. And he'd felt her breath whisper over his mouth. It had taken more effort than he liked to admit to pull back and deny himself the need he'd had to take her face in his hands, angle her mouth for better access so he could explore her with a thoroughness that would have made him look a complete fool...

Cruz only became aware that he was being watched when the hairs went up on the back of his neck, and he turned his head from brooding out of the small window. He had to adjust his gaze down to see that one of his nephews—he couldn't tell which—was standing by his chair with small pudgy hands clutching the armrest.

For a second time was suspended, and his mind went blank. Two huge dark eyes stared up at him guilelessly. Thick, dark tousled hair fell onto a smooth forehead and the child's cheeks were flushed. Something that looked like mashed carrot was smeared around his mouth. And then he smiled, showing a neat row of baby teeth. Something gripped Cruz tight in his chest, throwing him back in time to when he'd looked at an almost identical child, six years his junior.

'*Matty*, don't disturb your uncle.'

That low, husky voice. Gently chiding. Two slender pale hands came around his nephew to lift him up and away. Trinity held him easily with one arm, against her body. The small face showed surprise, and then started to contort alarmingly just before an ear-splitting screech emerged.

Cruz noted that she looked slightly frayed at the edges. Her hair was coming loose and she had smears of food on her jacket. He looked down and saw pale bare feet, nails painted a delicate shade of coral, and he felt a surge of blood to his groin. Immediately he scowled at his rampant reaction and Trinity backed away.

'Sorry, I didn't realise he'd slipped out of his chair.'

She was turning to walk back down the plane when Cruz heard himself calling out, 'Wait.'

She stopped in her tracks and Cruz saw Mrs Jordan hurrying up the aisle, reaching for Mateo to take him from Trinity. The indignant shouting stopped as the older woman hushed him with soothing tones.

Trinity turned around and Cruz felt something pierce him as he acknowledged that, *in*convenient wedding or not, most brides were at least given a meal before being whisked away after their nuptials.

They'd gone straight from his solicitor's office, where Trinity had signed the pre-nuptial agreement, to the register office and then to the plane. He'd expected her to pore over the pre-nuptial agreement, but she'd just glanced through it and then looked at him and said, 'If we divorce then I lose all custody of the boys, is that it?'

He'd nodded. Aware of his body humming for her even while they were surrounded by his legal team. She'd just muttered something under her breath like, *Never going to happen*, and signed. Cruz had had to include some kind of a severance deal for her if they divorced, so Trinity would always be a wealthy woman, but he knew she could have fought him for a better deal.

So why hadn't she? asked a voice, and Cruz didn't like the way his conscience smarted. He wasn't used to being aware of his conscience, never doubting himself in anything—and he wasn't about to start, he told himself ruthlessly. For all he knew Trinity's actions thus far were all an act to lull him into a false sense of security.

'Have you eaten yet?' he asked abruptly, irritated that she was making him doubt himself.

She looked at him warily and shook her head as she tucked some hair behind her ear. 'I'll eat when the boys have eaten.'

Cruz gestured to the seat across the aisle from him. 'Sit down. I'll get one of the staff to take your order.' He pressed the call button.

Trinity looked towards the back of the plane for a moment. Her visible reluctance was not a reaction he was used to where women were concerned.

'Sit before you fall. They're fine. And we have some things to discuss.'

She finally sat down, just as an attentive air steward appeared and handed her a menu. Trinity's head was downbent for a moment as she read, and Cruz found it hard to look away from that bright silky hair.

When the air steward had left Trinity felt uncomfortable under Cruz's intense gaze. It was as if he was trying to get into her head and read her every thought. Just the prospect of that made her go clammy—that he might see the effect his very chaste kiss had had on her.

In a bid to defuse the strange tension, she prompted, 'You said we have things to discuss...?'

Cruz blinked and the intensity diminished. Trinity

sucked in a breath to acknowledge how attuned she felt to this man. It was disconcerting—and unwelcome.

'As soon as you're settled at the *castillo* I'll organise interviews for another nanny to help Mrs Jordan. You're going to be busy as my wife.'

The castillo. It even sounded intimidating. She said, as coolly as she could, as if this was all completely normal, 'Maybe this would be a good time for you to let me know exactly what you expect of me as your wife.'

Maybe, crowed a snide voice, *it would have been a good idea for you not to get so attached to two babies that aren't yours in a bid to create the family you never had.*

Trinity gritted her jaw.

Cruz said, 'My calendar is already full for the next three months, and I should warn you that my social events are more corporate-orientated than celebrity-based... I'll expect you on my arm, looking the part, and not scowling because you're bored.'

Trinity boiled inside. Clearly he was expecting her to last for about two weeks before she ran for the hills. And he was obviously referring to Rio's predilection for film premieres or events like the Monte Carlo Grand Prix, which Trinity had found excruciating—all she could remember of that particular event was the overwhelming diesel fumes and the constant seasickness she'd felt while on some Russian oligarch's yacht.

Rio had invariably paraded her in public and then promptly dropped her once the paparazzi had left—which had suited her fine. She'd usually been in her own bed, in her own separate room, by the time he'd finished partying around dawn. But she could just imagine telling Cruz that, and how he'd merely shut her down again.

Then she thought of something. 'What do you mean, "looking the part"?'

He swept an expressive look over her, and at that moment she was aware of every second of sleep she hadn't got in the past couple of years. *And* the fact that today was probably the first day she'd worn smart clothes and actually put on make-up in months.

Compounding her insecurity, Cruz said, 'As *my* wife you'll need to project a more…classic image. I've already arranged for you to be taken shopping to buy new clothes.'

Trinity tensed at the barb. 'But I have clothes.'

His lip curled. 'The kind of clothes you wore around my brother will not be suitable and they've been donated to charity.'

Her face grew hot when she recalled seeing Cruz again, for the first time since her marriage to Rio, three months ago. His effect on her had been instantaneous—a rush of liquid heat. And then he'd looked at her as if she was a call girl. How could she blame him? She'd felt like one.

Rio's sense of style for women had definitely favoured the 'less is more' variety. He'd handed her a dress to wear for that party that had been little more than a piece of silk. Skimpier than anything she'd ever worn.

She'd protested, but he'd said curtly, 'You're working for me, Trinity. Consider this your uniform.'

It hadn't been long after their row and her finding out exactly why he'd married her. Rio had been acting more edgily than usual, so Trinity hadn't fought him on the dress and had assured herself that she'd talk to Cruz that night—seek his help. Except it hadn't turned out as she'd expected. She'd been a fool to think she could turn to him.

The memory left her feeling raw. She averted her eyes from Cruz's now and said stiffly, 'It's your money—you can spend it as you wish.'

The air steward came back with Trinity's lunch, and she focused on the food to try and distract herself from a feeling of mounting futile anger and impotence. But the fact that she was destined to dance to the tune of another autocratic De Carrillo man left the food in her mouth tasting of dust.

She gave up trying to pretend she had an appetite and pushed her plate away. Cruz looked up from the small laptop he'd switched his attention to. He frowned with disapproval at how little she'd eaten—it was an expression that was becoming very familiar to Trinity, and one she guessed was likely to become even more familiar.

Her anger rose. 'Was this marriage really necessary?' she blurted out, before she could censor her tongue.

A bit late now, whispered that annoying voice.

As if privy to that voice, Cruz mocked, 'It really is futile to discuss something that's already done. But by all means, Trinity, feel free to seek a divorce whenever you want.'

And leave Matty and Sancho at this man's mercy? Never, vowed Trinity.

Just then a plaintive wail came from the back of the plane.

'Mummy!'

She recognised the overtired tone. Seizing her opportunity to escape, Trinity stood up and tried not to feel self-conscious in her creased dress and bare feet.

'Excuse me. I should help Mrs Jordan.'

She walked away with as much grace as she could muster and tried her best not to feel as though her whole world was shrinking down to the size of a prison cell—even if it was to be the most luxurious prison cell in the world.

A few hours later Trinity shivered, in spite of the warm Spanish breeze. They'd driven into a massive circular courtyard and she was holding a silent and wide-eyed Sancho in her arms, thumb stuck firmly in his mouth. Mrs Jordan was holding a similarly quiet Matty. They were still a little groggy after the naps they'd had on the plane.

Her instinct about the *castillo* being intimidating had

been right. It was massive and imposing. A mixture of architecture, with the most dominant influence being distinctly Moorish. Cruz had explained that they were about midway between Seville and a small historic town called El Rocio, which sat on the edge of a national park. But there was nothing around them now except for rolling countryside; he hadn't been lying about that.

Cruz was greeting some staff who had appeared in the imposing porch area. They were all dressed in black. Trinity caught Mrs Jordan's eye and was relieved to see that the older woman looked as intimidated as she felt.

Mrs Jordan said brightly, 'Well, my word, I don't think I've ever seen anything so grand. I'm sure it's bright and airy on the inside.'

But when they went in, after a whirlwind of introductions to several staff whose complicated names Trinity struggled to imprint on her brain, it wasn't bright and airy. It was dark and cool—and not in a refreshing way.

The stone walls were covered with ancient tapestries that all seemed to depict different gruesome battles. Then there were portraits of what had to be Cruz's ancestors. She could see where he got his austere expression. They all looked fearsome. There was one in particular whose resemblance to Cruz was uncanny.

She hadn't even noticed that she'd stopped to stare at it for so long until a cool voice from behind her said, 'That's Juan Sanchez De Carrillo—my great-great-grandfather.'

Unnerved, in case he might guess why she'd been momentarily captivated by the huge portrait, Trinity desisted from saying that she thought it looked like him. Instead she asked, 'So is this where you and Rio grew up?'

For a moment he said nothing, and Trinity looked at him. She caught a fleeting expression on his face that she couldn't read, but then it was gone.

He led her forward, away from the portrait, as he said

smoothly, 'Yes, we were both born in this *castillo*. But our circumstances couldn't have been more different.'

'I know,' Trinity said cautiously. 'Rio told me that his mother was a maid here, and that she blackmailed your father for money after their affair and then left Rio behind.'

In spite of everything that had happened, she *still* felt sympathy. These dark corridors and austere pictures only confirmed that Cruz's experience couldn't have been much happier here. That treacherous curiosity to know more rose up again, much to her disgust. She was a soft touch.

But Cruz was clearly not up for conversation. He was moving again, leaving the long corridor, and she had to follow or be left behind. He opened a door to reveal an enclosed open-air courtyard and Trinity automatically sucked in a deep breath, only realising then how truly oppressive the *castillo* had felt.

They'd lost Mrs Jordan and the other staff somewhere along the way. Afraid that Cruz suspected she was angling for a personal tour, she shifted Sancho's heavy and now sleeping weight on her shoulder and hurried after his long strides.

'You don't have to show me around—there'll be plenty of time for that.'

A whole lifetime, whispered that wicked voice.

Cruz just said brusquely, 'This isn't a tour. We're just taking another route to your quarters.'

Trinity felt a childish urge to poke her tongue out at his back. *Your quarters.* She shivered a little.

He led them back into the *castillo* on the other side of the surprisingly pretty courtyard. The sensation of the walls closing around her again made her realise that this was *it*. Hers and the boys' home for the foreseeable future. The prospect was intimidating, to say the least.

Trinity vowed then and there to do everything she could to ensure Matty and Sancho's happiness and security in such a dark and oppressive atmosphere. After all, she'd chosen to be their protector and she had no regrets.

Cruz helped himself to a shot of whisky from the sideboard in his study on the other side of the *castillo*. He took a healthy sip, relishing the burn which distracted him from the uncomfortable feeling that lingered after walking away from Trinity, Mrs Jordan and the boys, all looking at him with wide eyes, as if they'd just been transported to Outer Mongolia.

He didn't like the way his nephews fell silent whenever he approached them, looking at him so warily, clinging on to Trinity. His urge to protect them had grown exponentially since he'd decided marriage was the only option— thanks to which he was now their legal guardian too.

While the jury was still very much out on Trinity—her easy signing of the pre-nup had thrown up questions he wasn't eager to investigate—he had to admit grudgingly that so far it didn't look as if his nephews were being adversely affected by her.

Cruz had been surprised to discover that Rio had told her the full extent of his mother's treachery.

When he and Rio had been younger they'd never been allowed to play together, and on the few occasions Cruz had managed to sneak away from his nanny to find Rio his younger half-brother had always looked at him suspiciously.

One day they had been found together. Cruz's father had taken Rio into his study, and he could still remember the shouts of humiliation as his father had beaten him. Rio had eventually emerged with tears streaking his red face, holding his behind, glaring at Cruz with a hatred that had been vivid.

Their father had appeared in the doorway and said to Cruz, 'That's what'll happen if you seek him out again. His is *not* your real brother.'

Cruz had felt so angry, and yet so impotent. That was the moment he'd vowed to ensure that Rio was never denied what was rightfully his...much good it had done his brother in the end.

He realised now for the first time that the knowledge that he was his nephews' legal guardian had soothed something inside him. Something he never could have acknowledged before, while Rio had held him at arm's length. It was the part of him that had failed in being able to protect his brother when they were younger. He was able to do this now for his nephews in the most profound way. It made emotion rise up, and with it futile anger at Rio's death.

Cruz's mind deviated then, with irritating predictability, back to his new wife. He'd expected something more from her by now—some show or hint of defiance that would reveal her irritation at having her wings clipped. But there was nothing. Just those big blue eyes, looking at him suspiciously. As if he might take a bite out of her... That thought immediately made him think of sinking his teeth into soft pale flesh.

What the hell was wrong with him? He would not fall into that pit of fire again. She disgusted him.

A little voice jeered at him. *She disgusts you so much that your blood simmers every time she's close?*

Cruz shut it down ruthlessly.

Trinity would not tempt him again. This situation was all about containment and control and ensuring his nephews were in his care and safe. That was all that mattered— their legacy. As soon as she realised how limited her life would be she'd be begging for a divorce, and that day couldn't come soon enough.

CHAPTER FOUR

A WEEK LATER Trinity felt as if she were on a slightly more even keel. She and the boys and Mrs Jordan had finally settled, somewhat, into their palatial rooms. Decorated in light greys and soft pinks and blues, with contemporary furniture and a modern media centre, they made for a more soothing environment than the rest of the dark and brooding *castillo*, which was not unlike its owner.

Mrs Jordan had an entire apartment to herself, as did Trinity, and they were both connected by the boys' room, which was light and bright but other than that showed no indication that it was home to two small boys with more energy than a bag of long-life batteries.

They took their meals in a large sunny dining room, not far from their rooms, that led out to a landscaped garden. Trinity and Mrs Jordan spent most of their time running after Matty and Sancho, trying to stop them pulling the very exotic-looking flowers out of the pristine beds.

Trinity sighed now, and pushed some hair behind her ear as she contemplated the two napping toddlers who looked as exhausted as she felt. She'd have to talk to Cruz about modifying their bedroom and installing something more practical outside that would occupy their vast energy and satisfy their need to be stimulated. Otherwise the head gardener was going to be very upset, and the boys were going to grow more and more frustrated.

The staff they'd seen so far—a taciturn housekeeper who spoke no English and a young girl who looked terrified—hardly inspired confidence in it being a happy household where she could get to know people and let the boys run free. It was very obvious that Cruz believed he had corralled them exactly where he wanted them and had now all but washed his hands of her, in spite of his decree that she be available as his social escort.

Mrs Jordan had had the morning off, and was going to keep an eye on the boys this afternoon when they woke, so Trinity took the opportunity to go and see if Cruz had returned from his trip to Madrid yet—she'd managed to ascertain that he'd gone from the shy maid.

She refused to give in to a growing feeling of helplessness but while making her way from their wing of the *castillo*, back through the pretty courtyard, she could feel her heart-rate increasing. She told herself it was not in anticipation of seeing Cruz after a few days. What was wrong with her? Was she a complete masochist?

As she walked past the stern portraits of the ancestors she didn't look up, not wanting to see if their eyes would be following her censoriously, judging her silently.

Just at that moment a door opened and a tall hard body stepped out—right in front of Trinity. She found herself slamming straight into the man who so easily dominated her thoughts.

Big hands caught her upper arms to stop her lurching backwards. All her breath seemed to have left her lungs with the impact as she stared up into those tawny eyes.

Somehow she managed to get out the words, 'You're back.'

Cruz's hands tightened almost painfully on Trinity's arms. 'I got back late last night.'

Tension was instant between them, and something else much more ambiguous and electric. She tried to move back but she couldn't.

Panic that he might see her reaction to him spiked. 'You can let me go.'

Cruz's eyes widened a fraction, as if he'd been unaware he was holding her, and then suddenly he dropped his hands as if burnt. Trinity stepped back, feeling sick at the expression crossing his face—something between disgust and horror. She'd seen that look before, after he'd kissed her.

She said quickly, 'I was looking for you, actually.'

After a silent moment Cruz stepped aside and gestured for her to go into the room he'd just left. She stepped inside, still feeling shaky after that sudden physical impact.

Cruz closed the door and walked to his desk, turning around to face her. 'I'll call for some coffee—or would you prefer tea?'

'Tea would be lovely, thank you.'

So polite. As if he *hadn't* just dumped her and her stepsons in his remote intimidating home and left them to their own devices. Maybe he thought she would have run screaming by now?

When Cruz turned away to lean over his desk and pick up the phone Trinity had to consciously drag her gaze away from where his thin shirt stretched enticingly over flexed and taut muscles. She looked around the room, which was huge and obviously his home office.

Dark wood panelling and big antique furniture gave it a serious air. Floor-to-ceiling shelves dominated one whole wall, and Trinity felt a wave of heat scorch her from the inside out as the memory of another wall of shelves flashed back, of how it had felt to have Cruz press her against it so passionately.

'Do you still read?'

Trinity's head snapped back to Cruz. She hadn't even noticed that he'd finished the call. She was mortified, and crushed the memory, hoping her cheeks weren't flaming.

She shook her head, saying with a slightly strangled voice, 'I haven't had much time lately.' She was usually so exhausted when she went to bed now that her love of reading was a thing of the past. A rare luxury.

'Well? You said you were looking for me?'

He was looking at her expectantly, one hip resting on his desk, arms folded. Formidable. Remote. Her ex-employer, now her husband, but a stranger. It struck her then that even though they'd shared that brief intimacy, and she'd had a glimpse of what lay under the surface, he was still a total enigma.

She shoved down her trepidation. 'Yes. I wanted to talk to you about the boys.'

A light knock came on the door, and he called for whoever it was to come in as he frowned and said, 'What's wrong? Are they okay?'

The maid, Julia, appeared with a tray of tea and coffee, distracting Trinity. She noticed how the girl blushed when Cruz bestowed a polite smile on her and said thank you. Trinity felt humiliation curl inside her. She'd used to blush like that when she'd worked for him. It felt like a lifetime ago.

When the girl had left Cruz was still looking at Trinity, waiting for her answer. Feeling exposed under that laser-like intensity, she said, 'Nothing is wrong with them—they're fine. Settling in better than I'd expected, actually.'

Some of the tension left Cruz's shoulders and she felt a dart of unexpected emotion—what if he really did care about the boys?

He deftly poured tea for her and coffee for him and handed her a cup. 'Sit down.'

She chose a chair near the desk and cradled her cup, watching warily as he took a seat on the other side of his desk. He took a sip of his coffee and arched one dark golden brow, clearly waiting for her to elaborate.

She put the cup down on the table in front of her and sat up straight. 'The rooms…our rooms…are lovely. And very comfortable. But the boys' room isn't exactly tailored for children their age. It could do with brightening up, being made more cheerful—somewhere they can play and where they'll want to go to sleep. Also, they've been playing in the gardens—which they love—but again it's not exactly suitable for them. Your head gardener has already had to replant some of his flowerbeds.'

Cruz's conscience pricked as he acknowledged that he'd not even had the courtesy to stick around for one day and make sure that Trinity and his nephews and their nanny were comfortable.

He knew that the *castillo* was dated in parts, but the rooms he'd given to them had been those used by his mother before her death, so they were the most up-to-date. But evidently not up-to-date enough.

It hadn't even occurred to him to make the space child-friendly, and that stung now. What also stung was the fact that he had to acknowledge that his trip to Madrid had been less about business and more about putting some space between him and this new domestic world he'd brought back to Spain with him.

He was distracted by Trinity's very earthy clean-faced appeal. A look he had thought she'd eschewed as soon as she'd married Rio. Certainly any pictures he'd seen of them together had shown her to have morphed into someone who favoured heavy make-up and skimpy clothes.

And yet where was the evidence of that now? Her hair was pulled back into a low, messy bun. She was wearing soft jeans and a loose shirt, with a stain that looked suspiciously like dried food on her shoulder—as unalluring as any woman who had ever appeared in front of him, and yet it didn't matter. Cruz's blood sizzled over a low-banked fire of lust.

'So, what are you suggesting?' he asked, irritated at this reminder of how much she affected him.

Trinity swallowed, making Cruz notice the long slim column of her throat. Even that had an effect on him. *Damn it.*

'I'd like to make the boy's room more colourful and fun. And with regards to the garden… I'm not saying that that's not enough for them—your grounds are stunning—but they're bright, inquisitive boys and they're already becoming frustrated with being told they can't roam freely and touch what they want. Perhaps if they had something that would occupy their energy, like swings… They loved the children's playground in Regent's Park.'

All of what she'd just said was eminently reasonable, yet Cruz felt a tide of tension rising up through his body.

'Anything else?'

As if she could sense his tension, something flashed in her eyes. Fire. It sent a jolt of adrenalin through Cruz. She certainly wasn't the shy girl who'd come for that job interview a couple of years ago. More evidence of her duality, if he'd needed it.

She lifted her chin. 'Yes, actually. I don't know how the school systems work here, but if it's anything like in the UK I'll—' She stopped herself and flushed slightly. 'That is, *we'll* have to think about enrolling them in a local school. Also, I'd like to investigate playschools in the area—they should be around other children their own age. Surely you weren't expecting to them to never go beyond the *castillo* gates?'

He'd never been allowed beyond the *castillo* gates until he'd gone to boarding school in England.

He reacted testily to the fact that she was showing a level of consideration for his nephews that he'd never expected to see. 'Are you sure you're not just looking for opportunities to spread your own wings beyond these walls? You're not a prisoner, Trinity, you can leave any time you want. But if you do the boys remain here.'

She paled dramatically, any bravado gone, but seconds later a wash of bright pink came into her cheeks. Cruz was momentarily mesmerised by this display of emotion— he was used to people disguising their natural reactions around him. It had intrigued him before and he was surprised that she still had the ability.

She stood up. 'I'm well aware that I am here because I have little or no choice—not if I want to see my stepsons flourish and be secure—but I will never walk away from them. Not while they need me. I will do whatever it takes to ensure their happiness and wellbeing.'

Her blue eyes blazed. *Dios*, but she was stunning.

'So if you're hoping to see the back of me it won't be any time soon, I can assure you.'

With that, she turned on her heel and stalked out of the room, the heavy door closing with a solid *thunk* behind her. Cruz cursed volubly and stood up, muscles poised to go after her. But then he stopped.

He turned to face the window, which took in the breathtaking vista of the expanse of his estate. He couldn't allow Trinity to distract him by fooling him into thinking she'd changed. Because the moment he dropped his guard she'd have won.

'What on earth did you say to him?'

Trinity was too shocked to respond to Mrs Jordan's question as she took in the scene before her. Building was underway on a playground for the boys...an exact replica of the playground in Regent's Park.

At that moment the atmosphere became charged with a kind of awareness that only happened around one person. *Cruz.*

Mrs Jordan reacted to his presence before Trinity did. 'Mr De Carrillo, this really is spectacular—the boys will love it.'

He came to stand beside Trinity and his scent tickled her nostrils, earthy and masculine. Her belly tightened and she flushed. Superstitiously she didn't want to look at him, as if that might make his impact less.

He answered smoothly, 'Please, Mrs Jordan, call me Cruz... Trinity was right—the boys need somewhere they can expend their energy safely.'

Matty and Sancho were currently playing with big toy building bricks in an area that had been cordoned off for them by the builders. They were wearing small hard hats and jeans and T-shirts and they looked adorable, faces intent, trying to keep up with the real builders just a few feet away.

Mrs Jordan turned to Cruz more directly and said, with an innocent tone in her voice, 'We were just about to bring the boys in for lunch—won't you join us?'

Trinity glanced at the woman, aghast, but Mrs Jordan was ignoring her. Fully expecting Cruz to refuse, she couldn't believe it when, after a long moment, he said consideringly, 'Thank you. That would be lovely.'

Mrs Jordan smiled. 'I'll ask Julia to add another place.'

She disappeared with a suspicious twinkle in her eye before Trinity could say anything. She supposed she couldn't really blame the woman for taking the opportunity to meddle gently when it arose.

When Trinity glanced up at Cruz she almost expected him to look irritated at the thought of spending lunch with them, but he was staring at the boys with an enigmatic expression on his face. Uncertainty?

Then, as if he sensed her watching him, the expression was gone and he looked down at her. 'You haven't said anything—are the plans all right?'

Against her best intentions to remain impervious to this man's pull, something inside her melted a little at

his thoughtfulness. She forced a smile. 'They're perfect.
I didn't expect you to take my words so literally.'

He frowned. 'But you said they loved that playground,
so naturally I would try to recreate it for them.'

Trinity desisted from pointing out that only a billionaire would think along such lavish lines and just said dryly,
'It's extremely generous, and they will love it. Thank you.'

Cruz looked away from her to the boys and another curious expression crossed his face. She'd seen it before when
he looked at them: something between fear and longing.
Trinity cursed herself for not reading it properly till now.
This man scrambled her brain cells too easily.

She said, 'They won't bite, you know. They're as curious about you as you are about them.'

Without taking his eyes off them Cruz said gruffly,
'They always seem to look at me as if they don't know
what I am.'

Trinity felt something weaken inside her at this evidence of rare vulnerability. 'They don't really know you
yet, that's all. Once they become more used to you they'll
relax. Why don't you help me get them in for lunch?'

She moved forward before he could see how easily he
affected her.

'Matty! Sancho!' she called out when she came near
to where they were playing so happily. 'Time to go in for
lunch.'

Two identical faces looked up with predictable mulish-
ness—and then they spied Cruz and immediately put down
what they were playing with to come to Trinity. She bent
down to their level and took their hats off, ruffling their
heads, feeling the heat from their small, sturdy bodies.
Even though they were in the shade the Spanish spring
was getting warmer every day.

Cruz was towering over them in one of his trademark
pristine suits. No wonder he intimidated the boys. He in-

timidated her. Softly she said, 'It might help if you come down to their level.'

He squatted down beside her and the movement made her uncomfortably aware of his very potent masculinity. She closed her eyes for a second. What was wrong with her? Until she'd shared that incendiary moment with him in his study she'd had no great interest in sex. And yet a couple of days in Cruz's company again and all her hormones seemed to have come back to life.

She focused her attention on her boys, who were huddled close, brown eyes huge. 'Matty, Sancho...you know this is your Uncle Cruz's house, where we're going to live from now on?' She ignored the pang inside her when she said that, and the thought of a life stretching ahead of her as a wife of inconvenience.

'Man. The big man,' Matty observed.

Trinity bit back a smile at the innocent nickname. 'Yes, sweetie—but he's also your uncle and he wants to get to know you better.'

Sancho said nothing, just regarded his uncle. Then he said imperiously, 'Play with us.'

Matty jumped up and down. 'Yes! Play!'

Sensing things starting to unravel, Trinity said firmly, 'First lunch, and then you can play again for a little while.'

She scooped up Matty and handed him to Cruz, who took him awkwardly and rose to his feet. She then picked up Sancho and started to walk inside, almost afraid to look behind her and see how Matty must be tarnishing Cruz's sartorial perfection.

He was saying excitedly, 'Higher, Unkel Cooz...higher!'

Seeing his brother in the arms of the tall, scary man who now wasn't so scary was making Sancho squirm to get free from Trinity's arms. 'I want higher too!'

They walked into the bright dining room where Mrs Jordan was waiting for them. Trinity didn't miss the gleam of approval in the woman's eyes when she saw Cruz carrying one of his nephews.

Trinity thought again of that rare chink of vulnerability Cruz had revealed outside. She realised belatedly that this had to be hard for him—coming from such a dark and dour place with only a half-brother he'd never been allowed to connect with properly. And yet he was making a real effort.

A rush of tenderness flooded her before she could stop it.

She tried to hide her tumultuous emotions as she strapped Sancho into his high seat. When she felt composed again she looked up to see Mrs Jordan showing Cruz how to strap Mateo into his. He looked flummoxed by such engineering, and it should have emasculated the man but it didn't. It only made that tenderness surge again. Pathetic.

Cruz sat down at the head of the table. The boys were seated one on each side beside Trinity and Mrs Jordan. Staff scurried in and out, presenting a buffet of salads and cold meats, cheese and bread. The boys were having chopped up pasta and meatballs. They ate with their habitual gusto, insisting on feeding themselves and invariably spraying anyone in close proximity with tiny bits of pasta and meat.

Trinity sneaked another glance at Cruz to see if this domestic milieu was boring him, but he was watching his nephews, fascinated.

'How do you tell them apart?' he asked, during a lull when small mouths were full.

Trinity nodded her head towards Mateo on the other side of the table. 'Matty is a tiny bit taller and leaner. He's also a little more gregarious than Sancho. Where he leads, Sancho follows. She scooped some of Sancho's food back onto his plate and said with a fond smile, 'Sancho is more watchful and quiet. He's also got a slightly different coloured right eye—a tiny discolouration.'

Cruz leaned forward to look and Sancho grinned at the attention, showing tiny teeth and a mouth full of masticated food.

When he pulled back, Cruz said a little faintly, 'Rio had the same thing…one eye was slightly lighter in colour.'

'He did…?' Trinity had never noticed that detail.

Cruz sent her a sharp glance and she coloured and busied herself cleaning up Sancho's tray, feeling absurdly guilty when she had no reason to. It wasn't as if she'd spent any time looking deep into Rio's eyes. Not that Cruz would believe that. She wondered if he ever would.

It didn't escape her notice that Mrs Jordan had excused herself on some flimsy pretext. Trinity sighed inwardly. She wouldn't put it past the woman, who subsisted on a diet of romance novels, to try and matchmake her and Cruz into a real marriage.

The thought of that was so absurd that she coloured even more for a moment, as if Cruz might see inside her head.

The very notion of this man looking at her with anything other than suspicious disdain was utterly inconceivable.

But he looked at you differently once before, said a little voice.

Trinity blocked it out. Cruz wouldn't touch her again if his life depended on it—of that she was sure. And that suited her just fine. If he ever discovered how susceptible she still was—*and* how innocent she still was, in spite of his belief that her marriage to Rio had been a real one… The thought sent a wave of acute vulnerability through her.

Cruz's comprehensive rejection of her had left a wound in a deeply private feminine space. The thought of opening herself up to that rejection again was terrifying.

Cruz cleared his throat then, and said, 'I've arranged

for you to be taken to a local boutique tomorrow morning, where a stylist will help you choose a wardrobe of clothes. Think of it as a trousseau.'

Trinity put down the napkin and looked at him. She felt raw after her recent line of thinking. She hated to be so beholden to him. It made her feel helpless and she didn't like that. She saw the look in his eye, as if he was just waiting for her to show her true avaricious nature.

'There's not just me to think of,' she said testily. 'I need to get the boys some new clothes too, more suitable for this warmer climate. They're growing so fast at the moment that they've almost outgrown everything.'

Cruz inclined his head, only the merest glint in his eye showing any reaction to her spiky response. 'Of course. I should have thought of that. I'll see to it that the stylist takes you to a suitable establishment for children also.'

The boys were starting to get bored now, having eaten enough and grown tired of the lack of attention and activity. Sancho was already manoeuvring himself to try and slip out of his chair and Trinity caught him deftly.

She took advantage of the distraction. 'I'll let them play some more while their lunch digests and then it'll be time for their afternoon nap.'

Without asking for help, Cruz stood and plucked a clearly delighted Matty, little arms outstretched, out of his seat. It irked her no end that Cruz was already holding him with an ease that belied the fact that it was only the second time he'd held one of his nephews in his arms.

It suited him. Matty looked incredibly protected in those strong arms and a sharp poignancy gripped her for a moment as she realised that he was already charming them. They'd gone from looking at him as if he was about to devour them whole, to looking at him with something close to awe and adoration. Their tiny minds were obviously cottoning onto the fact that this tall person might become an important ally and be able to do things that Trinity and Mrs Jordan couldn't.

Sancho was whingeing—he wanted to be in the big man's arms too.

Cruz held out his other arm, 'I can take him.'

After a moment's hesitation Trinity handed him over, to see Cruz expertly balance Sancho in his other arm. And then he walked out of the room, two glossy brown heads lifted high against his chest. The twins were delighted with themselves, grinning at her over those broad shoulders.

And just like that Trinity knew she'd started to lose them to Cruz... And, as wrong as it was, she couldn't but help feel a tiny bit jealous at how easily he accepted the innocence of his nephews when he would never ever accept the possibility of Trinity's. Not while he was so blinded by his loyalty to his deceased brother.

The next few days passed in a blur for Trinity. She was taken to cosmopolitan and beautiful Seville by Cruz's driver, to a scarily exclusive boutique where she lost track of the outfits she tried on. Then she was taken to a department store that stocked children's clothes, where she picked up everything she needed for the boys.

Their bedroom had been refurbished, and once again Cruz's efficiency had been impressive. An interior designer had taken her ideas on board and now, with murals of animals and tractors and trains on the walls, it was a bright and inviting space for two small boys. And they each had a bed, built in the shape of a car.

For a moment, when she'd seen it transformed and the way the boys had stood there in wide-eyed awe, she'd felt ridiculously emotional. They would have so much more than she'd ever had...or even their father.

She would have thanked Cruz, but he hadn't been

around much in the last few days. He hadn't joined them for lunch again, and the boys had been asking for him plaintively.

Trinity folded up the last of Sancho and Matty's new clothes and put them in the colourful set of drawers, chastising herself for the constant loop in her head that seemed to veer back to Cruz no matter how hard she tried to change it.

She was about to push the drawer closed when a deep voice came from behind her. 'Where are the boys?'

She jumped and whirled around to see Cruz filling the doorway, dressed in jeans and a shirt open at the neck. Irritation at the way she'd just been wondering about him, and the effortless effect he had on her, made her say waspishly, 'They're outside, playing with Mrs Jordan.'

Her irritation only increased when she found herself noticing how gorgeous he looked.

'They've been asking for you, you know. If you're going to be in their lives you need to be more consistent. They don't understand why you're there one day but not the next…it confuses them.'

Her conscience pricked. What she really meant was that it put *her* on edge, not knowing where or when he was likely to turn up…

His gaze narrowed on her and he slowly raised one brow. Clearly the man wasn't used to having anyone speak to him like this. Well, tough, she told herself stoutly. She was no longer in awe of her scarily sexy stern boss. She folded her arms.

'I understand that you've had your wardrobe replenished, as well as my nephews'?' Cruz drawled.

Trinity flushed. She immediately felt churlish and unfolded her arms. 'I wanted to say thank you for the bedroom—it worked out beautifully, and the boys love it. And, yes, we got clothes… But more clothes were delivered from the boutique than I ever looked at or tried on…it's too much.'

Cruz shook his head slowly, a hard light in his eye. 'Still with the act? I'm impressed. I thought you would have cracked by now and shown your true colours—but perhaps you're saving yourself for a more appreciative audience.'

She just looked at him. This evidence of his continued mistrust hurt her and, terrified to look at why that was, and not wanting him to see her emotions, she focused on the last thing he'd said. 'What do you mean, *audience?*'

'I have a function to attend in Seville tomorrow night. It'll be our first public outing as husband and wife.'

Panic gripped her. 'But Mrs Jordan—'

Cruz cut her off. 'Has already agreed to babysit. And we're rectifying that situation next week. I've organised with a local recruitment agency for them to send us their best candidates for another nanny. It'll free you up to spend more time with me, and Mrs Jordan will have more of her own free time.'

'Is that really necessary?' she asked, feeling weak at the thought of more time with him.

'Yes.' Cruz sounded impatient now. 'I'll have social functions to attend and I expect you to be by my side. As discussed.'

Trinity's irritation flared again. and she welcomed it. 'As I recall it was more of a decree than a discussion.'

Cruz's jaw clenched. 'You can call it what you want. We both know that, thanks to Rio's dire financial state when he died, you had no way of offering independent support to my nephews without me. The sooner you accept this as your new reality, the easier it will be for all of us.'

And evidently Cruz still believed that state of financial affairs to be *her* fault, based on her alleged profligate spending of her husband's money.

For a moment Trinity wanted to blurt out the truth—that

Rio had hated Cruz so much he'd wanted to ruin him—but Cruz wouldn't believe her, and she found that the impulse faded quickly. First of all, it wasn't in her to lash out like that, just to score a point. And she also realised she didn't want to see the effect that truth would have on him, when he clearly believed that his brother had been flawed, yes, but inherently decent.

And that shook her to the core—knowing that she resisted wanting to hurt him. Even as he hurt her.

She had to take responsibility for the fact that she'd agreed to the marriage of convenience with Rio. She really had no one to blame but herself.

And, as much as she hated this situation and being financially dependent, she couldn't deny the immutable fact that Matty and Sancho were in the privileged position of being heirs to this great family legacy and fortune. She didn't have the right to decide on their behalf, even as their legal guardian, that she was going to fight to take them away from all this and turn their lives into something it didn't have to be.

The silence grew between them almost to breaking point, a battle of wills, until eventually Trinity said, 'Fine. What time do I need to be ready?'

There was an unmistakable gleam of triumph in Cruz's eyes now and he said, 'We'll leave at six. It's a formal event, so wear a long gown. I'll have Julia show you to the vaults so you can pick out some jewellery.'

Jewellery...vaults... Not wanting him to see how intimidated she was, or how easily he affected her emotions, she just said coolly, 'Fine. I'll be ready by six.'

CHAPTER FIVE

THE FOLLOWING EVENING Cruz paced back and forth in the entrance hall of the *castillo* and looked at his watch again impatiently. He forced himself to take a breath. It was only just six o'clock so Trinity wasn't actually late *yet*. Just then he heard a sound and looked to where she stood at the top of the main stairs.

For a long second he could only stare, struck dumb by the glittering beauty of the woman in front of him. She was refined...elegant. Classic. Stunning.

Her dress was long—as he'd instructed—and a deep blue almost navy colour. It shone and glistened and clung to those impossibly long legs, curving out to her hips and back in to a small waist. It shimmered as she came down the stairs. It clung everywhere—up over her torso to where the material lovingly cupped full, perfectly shaped breasts. All the way to the tantalising hollow at the base of her throat.

Cruz was dimly aware that he'd possibly never seen less flesh revealed on a woman, and yet this dress was sexier than anything he'd ever seen in his life. Her hair was pulled back at the nape of her neck, highlighting the delicate slim column of her throat and her bone structure.

She gestured to herself and he could see that she was nervous.

'What is it? Is the dress not suitable?'

Cruz realised he was ogling. He felt a very uncharacteristic urge to snap, *No, the dress is entirely unsuitable*. And yet that would be ridiculous. The dress effectively covered her from head to toe and he was reacting like an animal in heat—how the hell would he react when he saw some flesh? As it was, all the blood in his body was migrating from his brain to between his legs with alarming speed.

Any delusion he'd been under that he could successfully block out his awareness of this woman was laughable. She was under his skin, in his blood, and he couldn't deny it. His intellect hated this desire for her but his body thrummed with need.

Calling on all the control and civility he possessed, Cruz locked eyes with Trinity's—not that that helped. The colour of the dress only made her bright blue eyes stand out even more. They were like light sapphires, stunning and unusual.

'It's fine,' he said tightly. And then, goaded by thoughts of how she'd dressed for Rio, he said provocatively, 'Or perhaps you'd feel more comfortable in less material?'

To his surprise he saw the faintest shudder pass through her body. 'No. I never felt comfortable in the clothes Rio wanted me to wear.'

He looked at her. For some reason that admission only made him feel more conflicted.

Tersely he said, 'The driver is waiting—we should go.'

He indicated for her to precede him out of the *castillo* and his gaze tracked down her back and snagged on the enticing curves of her buttocks. He cursed himself. He was behaving as if he'd never seen a beautiful woman before in his life.

The driver helped her into the back of the luxury Jeep and Cruz got in the other side. As they were pulling out of the *castillo* courtyard his gaze swept over her again and he noticed something. 'You're not wearing any jewellery. Didn't you go to the vaults?'

She looked at him and Cruz saw a flush stain her cheeks. 'I did, but everything was so valuable-looking I was afraid to take anything.'

Something dark pierced him—was this finally evidence of her avaricious methods? Was this how she angled for more?

'Perhaps you'd have preferred something from Cartier or Tiffany's?'

She shook her head, eyes flashing. 'No, I wouldn't prefer that.' She held out her hand. 'I'm wearing the wedding band—isn't that enough? Or maybe you'd prefer if I wore a diamond-studded collar with a lead attached so no one is mistaken as to whom I belong?'

Irritation vied with frustration that she was so consistently refusing to conform to what he expected. He curtly instructed his driver to turn around and go back to the *castillo*.

'Why are we going back?' Trinity asked.

Cruz looked straight ahead. 'We're going back to get you an engagement ring.'

'I don't need one,' she said stubbornly.

He looked at her. 'It's not a choice. People will expect you to have a ring.'

She rounded on him, tense and visibly angry. 'Oh, and we can't have anyone suspecting that this isn't a real marriage, can we? Do you really think an engagement ring will convince people that you fell in love with your brother's widow?'

Cruz wanted to laugh at her suggestion of anyone in his circle ever being convinced that people married for love, but for some reason the laugh snagged in his chest.

'Don't be ridiculous,' he breathed, his awareness of her rising in an unstoppable wave in the confined space. 'No one would expect that. They'll know I'm protecting what's mine—my heirs.'

'And I'm just the unlucky pawn who got in your way.'

The bitterness in Tiffany's voice surprised him. Anger spiked at the way his control was starting seriously to fray at the edges. 'You put yourself in the way—by seducing my brother. By inserting yourself into my nephews' lives so they'd come to depend on you.'

She went pale and looked impossibly wounded. 'I've told you—that's not—'

Before she could issue another lie Cruz's control snapped and he acted on blind instinct and need. He reached for Trinity, clamping his hands around her waist, and pulled her towards him, vaguely registering how slender and light she felt under his hands.

He only had a second of seeing her eyes widen with shock before his mouth crashed down onto hers, and for a long second nothing existed except this pure, spiking shard of lust, so strong that he had no option but to move his mouth and haul Trinity even closer, until he could feel every luscious curve pressed against him.

And it was only in that moment, when their mouths were fused and he could feel her heart clamouring against his chest, that he could finally recognise the truth: he'd been aching for this since the night he'd kissed her for the first time.

Trinity wasn't even sure what had happened. A minute ago she'd been blisteringly angry with Cruz and now she was drowning and burning up at the same time. The desire she'd hoped she could keep buried deep inside her was shaming her with its instant resurrection. Brought back to life by a white-hot inferno scorching along every artery and vein in her body.

Cruz's mouth was hot and hard, moving over hers with such precision that Trinity couldn't deny him access, and when his tongue stroked hers with an explicitness that made heat rush between her legs her hands tightened around his arms, where they'd gone instinctively to hang on to something…anything…so she wouldn't float away.

His hands were still on her waist and one started moving up her torso, until it came tantalisingly close to the side of her breast, where her nipple peaked with need, stiffening against the sheer material of her underwear and her dress. She remembered what it was like to have his mouth on her there…the hot sucking heat…the excruciating pleasure of his touch.

A voice from the past whispered through the clamour of her blood—his voice. *'It should never have happened.'* It was like a slap across the face.

Trinity jerked backwards away from Cruz. She was panting as if she'd just run a race. Mortification was swift and all-consuming. He'd barely had to touch her before she'd gone up in flames. Any hope of convincing him she didn't want him was comprehensively annihilated. It wasn't even a comfort to see that his hair was dishevelled and his cheeks were flushed.

Those amber eyes glittered darkly. He muttered, 'I told myself I wouldn't touch you ever again, but I can't *not* touch you.'

She took her hands off him, but he caught them and held them tightly. The recrimination on his face was far too painfully familiar. She was angry and hurt.

'So now it's justifiable for you to kiss me, even if you still hate yourself for it? Because I'm your wife and not just a lowly maid?'

She pulled her hands free and balled them into fists in her lap.

Cruz frowned, 'What the hell are you talking about—justifiable?'

Trinity tried not to sound as emotional as she felt. 'You rejected me that night because you couldn't bear the thought that you'd kissed your maid. I saw the kind of women you took as lovers, and you don't need to tell me that I was nowhere near their level—socially, economically or intellectually.'

Cruz clamped his hands around her arms, his face flushing. He was livid. 'You think I stopped making love to you because I was a snob? *Dios* Trinity, that was *not* the case. I had to stop because you were my employee and I had a duty of care towards you. I put you in a compromising situation where you might have felt too scared to say no.'

His mouth twisted.

'My father was renowned for his affairs—some of which were with willing and impressionable staff members at the *castillo*. I vowed that I would never follow his footsteps—not least because I'd seen the destruction one of his affairs cost us all. He slept with Rio's mother, who took advantage of the situation, only to then abandon her son.'

Trinity was speechless for a moment as she absorbed this. 'You think,' she framed shakily, 'that I'm like Rio's mother, then? That I'm no better...?'

Cruz's wide, sensual mouth compressed. 'I didn't think so at first—not that night. I hated myself for losing control like that, but I didn't blame you. Since then...let's just say any illusions about your innocence I may have had have been well and truly shattered.'

An awful poignancy gripped Trinity at the thought that for a short while Cruz *had* seen the real her...and respected her. But the memory of her naivety and humiliation couldn't stop her saying bitterly, 'It would only have ever been a mistake, though, wouldn't it? I mean, let's not fool ourselves that it would have developed into anything... more...'

More. Like the kind of more that Cruz had once hoped existed until any such notion was drummed out of him by his mother and her bitter words? Since then he'd never been proved wrong—any woman he'd been with had only confirmed his cynicism. Not least this one. And yet... when he'd first laid eyes on her he'd never seen anyone who looked so untouched and innocent.

And she was looking at him now with those huge eyes, taunting him for his flight of fancy. It was as if she was reaching inside him to touch a raw wound.

He was unaware of his hands tightening on her arms, knew only that he needed to push her back.

'More...like what?' he all but sneered. 'Hearts and flowers? Tender lovemaking and declarations of undying love? I don't *do* tender lovemaking, Trinity, I would have taken you until we were both sated and then moved on. I have no time for relationships—my life isn't about that. It never was and it never will be. I have a duty of care to my nephews now, and you're here only because I'm legally bound to have you here.' His mouth twisted. 'The fact that I want you is a weakness I'm apparently not capable of overcoming.'

A veritable cavalcade of emotions crossed Trinity's face, and then a look of almost unbelievable hurt—it had to be unbelievable—superseded them all. She shrank back, pulling herself free, and he only realised then how hard he'd been holding her. He curled his hands into fists and cursed himself. What was it about this woman that made his brain fuse and cease functioning?

In a low voice that scraped along all of Cruz's raw edges she said, 'I wasn't looking for anything more than a book that night, no matter what you choose to believe.'

Cruz still felt volatile, and even more so now at this protestation of innocence and her stubborn refusal to reveal her true nature. He ground out, 'Maybe if I'd taken you as I'd wanted to, there against the bookshelves, we wouldn't be here now and Rio would still be alive.'

Trinity had thought he couldn't hurt her much more than he already had, but he just had—even as a lurid image blasted into her head of exactly the scenario he mentioned...his powerful body holding her captive against a wall of books while he thrust up, deep into her body.

She held herself rigid, denying that hurt, and blasted back, 'So you would have thrown over that elegant brunette beauty for me? Am I supposed to be flattered that you would have been happy to conduct an affair on your terms, only to discard me by the wayside when you were done with me?'

A muscle ticked in Cruz's jaw but he just said tersely, 'We're back at the *castillo*, we should get the ring. We've wasted enough time.'

Wasted enough time.

Trinity was still reeling as she followed Cruz's broad tuxedoed form down stone steps to the vaults, holding her dress up in one hand. The depth of his cynicism astounded her all over again, and she hated it that he'd hurt her so easily.

She blamed his interaction with Matty and Sancho. It had made her lower her guard against him and he'd punished her for it, reminding her that he was not remotely someone to pin her hopes and dreams on... She scowled at herself. Since when had she ever entertained those notions herself? It wasn't as if she'd ever been under any delusions of *more*.

More existed for people who weren't her or Cruz. Who had grown up with normal, functioning, loving families. And yet she couldn't deny that when she'd worked for him for a brief moment she'd entertained daydreams of him noticing her...wanting her...smiling at her—

Trinity slammed a lid on that humiliating Pandora's box.

She wasn't sure what was worse—finding out that Cruz hadn't dismissed her because she was a nobody all those years ago, or believing that if he'd taken her *until they were both sated* he could have averted Rio's destruction. Right now, she hated Cruz with a passion that scared her.

But not far under her hatred was something much more

treacherous. A very illicit racing excitement at the knowledge that he still wanted her. And that he'd rejected her because he'd felt he'd taken advantage of his position, not because he'd been horrified to find himself attracted to her...

Once in the vault, Trinity welcomed the change of scenery from the heightened and heated intensity of the back of the Jeep even as she shivered in the cold, dank air.

She hated herself for it, but found herself instinctively moving closer to Cruz's tall, lean form because the place gave her the creeps. She could imagine it being used as a location for the Spanish Inquisition, with its dark stone walls and shadowy cavernous corridors.

She thought, not a little hysterically, that if they'd been back in medieval times Cruz might have just incarcerated her down here in a cell.

He had pulled out a velvet tray of rings from a box in the wall and stood back. 'Choose one.'

Trinity reluctantly stepped forward. Almost immediately one ring in the centre of the tray caught her eye. It was one of the smallest rings, with an ornate gold setting and a small square ruby in the middle.

Cruz followed her gaze and picked it up. 'This one?'

She nodded. He took her hand and held it up and slid the ring onto her finger. It was a perfunctory gesture, so it shouldn't feel in any way momentous but it did. The ring fitted like a glove and, bizarrely, Trinity felt emotion rising when emotion had no place there—especially not after what had just passed between them.

Swallowing the emotion with effort, Trinity was unprepared when Cruz took her chin in his thumb and forefinger, tipping it up. The look in his eyes burned.

'As much as I'd like to be able to resist you, I don't think I can.'

Her heart thumped—hard. The thought of Cruz touching her again and seeing right through to where she was most vulnerable was anathema.

She jerked her chin out of his hand. 'Well, I can resist you enough for both of us.'

He smiled urbanely and stood back, putting out a hand to let her go ahead of him up the stairs and out of the vaults. 'We'll see,' he said with infuriating arrogance as she passed him, and she had to stop herself from running up the stairs, away from his silky threat.

This was Cruz's first social appearance back in Seville. His return was triumphant, now he had tripled his family's fortune and restored the reputation of the once great bank. Now no one would dare say to his face or behind his back the things they'd used to say when his father had been alive.

And yet he could not indulge in a sense of satisfaction. He was too keyed-up after that white-hot explosion of lust in the back of the Jeep, which had proved to him that where Trinity was concerned he had no control over his desires.

His body still throbbed with sexual frustration. And he was distracted by their exchange, and how it had felt to see her with that ring on her finger down in the vaults. It had affected him in a place he hadn't welcomed. As if it was somehow *right* that she should wear one of his family's heirlooms.

Down in that vault it had suddenly been very clear to him that he couldn't fight his desire for her—so why should he? He might not like himself for his weakness but she was his wife, and the prospect of trying to resist her for the duration of their marriage was patently ridiculous.

But something niggled at him—why wasn't she using his desire for her as a means to negotiate or manipulate? Instead she'd looked almost haunted when she'd fled up the steps from the vault. She was still pale now, her eyes huge. Irritation prickled across Cruz's skin. Maybe now that she knew he wanted her she was going to play him in a different way, drive him mad…

'What is it?' he asked abruptly. 'You look paler than a wraith.'

She swallowed, the movement drawing Cruz's gaze to that long, slender column. Delicate. Vulnerable. Damn her. She *was* just playing him. He was giving in to his base desires again and—

'I'm fine. I just… Events like this are intimidating. I never get used to it. I don't know what to say to these people.'

Cruz's recriminations stopped dead. If she was acting then she was worthy of an award. He had a vivid flash-back to seeing her standing alone in the crowd at that party in his house, the night of the accident, her stunning body barely decent in that scrap of a dress.

Cruz had been too distracted by the rush of blood to his extremities to notice properly. He'd hated her for making him feel as if he was betraying his brother by still feeling attracted to her. But the memory jarred now. Not sitting so well with what he knew of her.

Almost without registering the urge, Cruz took his hand off her elbow and snaked it around her waist, tugging her into his side. It had the effect of muting his desire to a dull roar. She looked up at him, tense under his arm. Something feral within him longed for her to admit to this at-traction between them.

'What are you doing?'

'We're married, *querida*, we need to look it. Just follow my lead. most of the people here are committed egotists, so once you satisfy their urge to talk about themselves they're happy.'

'You don't count yourself in that category?'

Her quick comeback caused Cruz's mouth to tip up.

Suddenly the dry, sterile event wasn't so...boring. And she had a flush in her face now, which aroused him as much as it sent a tendril of relief to somewhere she shouldn't be affecting him.

He replied dryly, 'I find it far more fruitful to allow others to run their mouths off.'

Cruz's hand rested low on Trinity's hip and he squeezed it gently.

She tensed again, as someone approached them, and he said, 'Relax.'

Relax...

It had been the easiest thing and the hardest thing in the world to melt into his side, as if she was meant to be there. It was a cruel irony that she seemed to fit there so well, her softer body curving into his harder form as if especially made for that purpose.

Cruz hadn't let her out of his orbit all night. Even when she'd gone to the bathroom as soon as she'd walked back in to the function room his eyes had been the first thing she'd seen, compelling her back to his side like burning beacons.

It had been both disconcerting and exhilarating. In social situations before she'd invariably been left to fend for herself, Rio being done with her once their initial entrance had been made.

Trinity sighed now and finished tucking Matty and Sancho into their beds—she'd come straight here upon their return from the function, all but running away from Cruz, who had been lazily undoing his bow tie and looking utterly sinful.

The boys were spreadeagled, covers askew, pyjamas twisted around their bodies. Overcome with tenderness for these two small orphaned boys, she smoothed back a lock of Sancho's hair and sat on the side of Matty's bed, careful not to disturb him. Resolve filled her anew not to bow under Cruz's increasingly down-and-dirty methods to disturb her—that incendiary kiss in the back of his Jeep, his words of silky promise in the vault…

After this evening things had changed. Cruz had obviously given himself licence to seduce her. And she knew if he touched her again her ability to resist would be shamefully weak.

She looked at the ring on her finger—heavy, golden. A brand. And an unwelcome reminder of the emotion she'd felt when Cruz had pushed it onto her finger.

She hated it that he believed whatever lies Rio had told him about her so easily. She wasn't remotely mercenary or avaricious. She had remonstrated with Rio countless times over the amounts of money he was spending on her. But he hadn't wanted to know. He'd told her that they had a certain standard to maintain, and that she needed to educate herself about fashion, art, et cetera.

The prospect of a future in which Cruz refused to listen to her and wore down her defences until he found out about her innocence in the most exposing way possible filled Trinity with horror.

She stood up and left the room decisively. She had to at least try to make Cruz see that she wasn't who he thought she was. She would appeal to him rationally, without emotion and physical desire blurring the lines between them.

Above all, she had to make him see that the twins were and always had been her priority.

It was time to talk to her husband and make him listen to her.

'Come in.'

Trinity nearly lost her nerve at the sound of that deeply authoritative voice, but she refused to give in to it and pushed the door open. Cruz was sitting behind his desk, jacket off, shirtsleeves rolled up and the top of his shirt undone. There was a glass of something in his hand. He epitomised louche masculine sensuality.

He looked up from the papers he'd been perusing and immediately sat up straight and frowned when he saw it was her. 'What's wrong? Is it the boys?'

His instant concern for his nephews heartened something inside her. Some fledgling and delicate hope that perhaps she *could* appeal to him. In spite of all the evidence so far to the contrary.

She shook her head. 'No, they're fine. I just checked on them.'

'Well, is it something else?'

Trinity came further into the room, suddenly aware that Cruz was looking at her with a very narrow-eyed assessing gaze and that she was still in the dress. She cursed herself for not having changed into something less...dramatic.

Cruz stood up. 'Would you like a drink?'

She shook her head, thinking that the last thing she needed was to cloud her brain. 'No, thank you.'

He gestured to a seat on the other side of the table and as she sat down he said, 'I noticed you didn't drink much earlier—you don't like it?'

She shook her head. 'Not really. I never acquired the taste.' As soon as she said that, though, she regretted not asking for some brandy—she could do with the Dutch courage.

'So? To what do I owe the pleasure of this late-night visit?'

Trinity looked at Cruz suspiciously. Something about the tone of his voice scraped across her jumping nerves. Was he mocking her for having exposed herself so easily earlier, when he'd kissed her? His expression was unreadable, though, and she told herself she was imagining things.

She took a breath. 'I just...wanted to talk to you about

this arrangement. About going forward, making a practical life together.'

Cruz took a sip of his drink and lowered the glass slowly again. 'Practical? I seem to recall events earlier which would turn the "practical" aspects of this relationship into far more pleasurable ones.'

Trinity immediately stood up, agitated. He *was* mocking her. 'I did not come here to talk about that.'

Totally unperturbed, and like a lazy jungle cat eyeing its prey, Cruz just sat back and said, 'Pity. What did you want to talk about, then?'

She ploughed on before this far more disturbing and *flirty* Cruz could make her lose her nerve.

'I know that I won't be able to continue with this sham marriage while you believe the worst of me and don't trust me. It'll start to affect the boys. They're too young to pick up on the tension now, but they're intelligent and inquisitive and it'll soon become apparent. That kiss earlier…it was unacceptable and disrespectful of my boundaries. This is meant to be a marriage in name only. You will either need to learn to deal with your antipathy for me or…' she took a breath '…we can move on from the past.'

Cruz went very still and then he put his glass down. He stood up and put his hands on the table, his eyes intense. A muscle ticked in his jaw. 'You think that kiss was a demonstration of my antipathy? That kiss was the inevitable result of our explosive mutual desire and proof that you want me as much as I want you.'

Trinity sucked in a breath, mortification rushing through her, and in a desperate bid to deny such a thing she blurted out, 'You gave me no time to respond. I was in shock.'

He arched a brow. 'So your response was down to shock?'

He stood up straight and started to move towards her.

Trinity panicked, stepping away from the chair. She should never have come in here. This had been a terrible idea.

'Yes,' she said desperately. 'Of course it was shock. And you can't do that… Just…manhandle me when you feel like it.'

Cruz stopped in his tracks. Trinity's words hung starkly in the air between them. Anger raced up his spine. No, *fury*. He had to control himself, because he was very close to *manhandling* her into admitting that their kiss had been very mutual.

But she was looking at him with wide eyes, as if he was some kind of wild mountain lion. He felt wild, and he was *not* wild. He was civilised.

He bit out, 'For someone being *manhandled* your response was very passionate.'

He saw her throat move as she swallowed and the pulse beating frantically at the base of her neck. Right now he knew with every cell in his body that if he was to touch her they would combust. But something held him back— some sense of self-preservation. He couldn't trust that she wasn't just baiting him on purpose.

When they did come together it would be on his terms, and he wouldn't be feeling these raw, uncontrolled urges pushing him to the limits of his control.

'Look,' she said, 'I'm here because there are things I want to talk to you about. Important things.'

Cruz kept his gaze up, away from her tantalising curves in that amazing dress. He would put nothing past her. One thing was for sure, though. She wasn't going to see how his blood throbbed just under the surface of his skin. He wouldn't lose it twice in one evening.

He leant back against his desk and folded his arms, as if that might stop him from reaching for her. 'Well, no one is stopping you from talking now, Trinity. I'm all ears.'

She swallowed visibly, and Cruz saw that she was nervous. Once again she could be taking advantage of this situation, seducing him, but she wasn't. It irritated him.

'All that stuff Rio told you about me being a gold-digger…none of it is true. He lied to you.'

Cruz went cold. She didn't have to come here and seduce him—she was smarter than that. She just had to come and mess with his head.

He stood and closed the distance between them and her eyes widened. He stopped just short of touching her. 'How dare you use the fact that my brother is silenced for ever as an excuse to further your own cause?'

'I'm not,' she said fiercely, tipping up her chin. 'You need to listen to me. You need to know the real truth of my marriage to Rio…'

A dark emotion was snapping and boiling inside Cruz at the thought of *the truth* of her marriage to Rio. Sharing his bed. The thought that his brother had got to fully taste what she'd offered up to Cruz so enticingly before he'd stopped her.

Did he want to hear about that? *No.* He wished that thoughts of her with Rio would make him turn from her in disgust, but the fire inside him only burnt brighter as he battled a primal urge to stake a claim that reduced him to an animal state.

He caught her arms in his hands and hauled her into his body, so he could remind her of where she was and with whom. *Him.*

He ground out, 'When will you get it that I will never trust a word you say? From now on if you want to try to manipulate me I'd prefer if you used the currency you use best…your body. At least that way we'll both get pleasure out of the interaction and it'll be a lot more honest.'

'Cruz…'

That was all he heard before he stopped Trinity's poisonous words with his mouth.

The kiss was an intense battle of wills. Cruz's anger was red-hot, thundering in his veins. But then she managed to break free, pulling back, her hands on his chest, breathing heavily. If Cruz had been able to call on any rationality he would have been horrified. No woman had ever driven him to such base urges. To want to stamp his brand on her.

They stared at each other, tension crackling. But then, as he looked down into those blue eyes, swirling with something he couldn't fathom, the intense anger dissipated to be replaced by something far less angry and more carnal.

He curled an arm around her waist, drawing her right in, close to his body, until he saw her cheeks flush with the awareness of his erection against her soft flesh. It was torture and pleasure all at once. With his other hand he reached around to the back of her head and undid her hair, so that it fell around her shoulders in a golden cloud.

He could feel her resistance melting. Even though she said, 'Cruz…don't…'

'Don't what?' he asked silkily. 'Do this?' And he touched her jaw, tracing its delicate line, then cupped her cheek, angling her head up.

She spread her hands on his chest and he thought she was going to push him away, but she didn't. Something inside him exulted. This time when he bent his head and kissed her there was an infinitesimal moment of hesitation and then her mouth opened to him and his blood roared. There was just *this,* and this was all that mattered right now.

CHAPTER SIX

TRINITY WAS RUNNING down the long, dark corridors of the *Castillo*. The stern faces of all those ancestors were staring down at her. each one silently judging her. The footsteps behind her were getting closer…her heart was in her throat, thumping so hard she could hardly breathe…

There was an open door on the left. She ducked in and slammed the door shut, chest heaving, sweat prickling on her skin. And then she heard it. The sound of breathing in the room…

Terror kept her frozen in place, her back to the door as the breathing got closer and closer. And then out of the gloom appeared a face. A very familiar, starkly beautiful face. Amber eyes hard. Stern. Angry. *Hot.*

Hands reached for her and Trinity knew she should try to escape. But suddenly she wasn't scared any more. She was excited… And instead of running she threw herself into Cruz's arms…

The disturbing dream still lingered, and Trinity shivered in the bright morning sunlight of another beautiful day. She didn't have to be a psychologist to figure out where it had come from. When Cruz had kissed her after that angry exchange in his study at first she'd resisted, but then something had changed…and when he'd touched her again she'd responded against her best intentions.

All the man had to do was touch her, look at her, and she wanted him. And with each touch and kiss it was getting harder to resist… She'd finally had the sense to pull back and step away last night, but it had taken every last shred of control she had.

Shakily she'd said, 'I didn't come here for this.'

'So you say,' Cruz had answered, with infuriating insouciance, looking as if he hadn't just kissed her so hard she could barely see straight. It had been particularly galling, because just moments before he'd demonstrated that once again any attempt to defend herself or tell the truth would be met with stubborn resistance.

A sense of futility made her ache inside. How could she continue like this? With Cruz blatantly refusing to listen to her? Maybe this was how he'd drive her away…by stonewalling her at every turn…

Matty shouted, 'Mummy, look! Unkel Cooz!'

Sancho jumped up, clapping his hands. 'Play, play!'

Trinity tensed all over as a long shadow fell over where she was sitting cross-legged in the grass; the boys were playing nearby. With the utmost reluctance she looked up, shading her eyes against Cruz's sheer masculine beauty as much as against the sun. Matty and Sancho—not scared of him at all any more—had grabbed a leg each, looking up at their new hero.

He lifted both boys up into his arms with an easy grace that annoyed her intensely. The fact that he was dressed down, in faded jeans and a dark polo shirt that strained across his chest muscles, was something she tried desperately not to notice. But it was hard when his biceps were bulging enticingly, reminding her of how it felt when they were wrapped around her.

She stood up, feeling at a disadvantage.

Cruz said, 'I came to tell you that I've been invited to another function this evening. We'll leave at seven.'

His autocratic tone sliced right into her, as did the scary prospect of countless more evenings like the previous one, when she'd reveal herself more and more. When he might *touch* her again.

She folded her arms and said coolly, 'I'm not going out this evening.'

The boys were squirming in Cruz's arms, growing bored already, and when he put them down they scampered off to the nearby sandpit. Trinity saw how his eyes followed them for a moment, making sure they were all right, and his concern made her feel warm inside until she clamped down on the sensation. This man evoked too much within her.

He looked back at her. 'I don't recall you being offered a choice.'

Irritation spiked at her reaction as much as to his tone. 'I'm not just some employee you can order around. It would be nice if you could pretend you're polite enough to *ask* if I'd like to come.'

'You're my wife,' Cruz offered tersely.

Something poignant gripped Trinity—if she was his wife for *real* then presumably they'd have a discussion about this sort of thing… She might agree to go because he'd tell her he'd be bored, or that he'd miss her if she didn't. The thought of that kind of domesticity made a treacherous shard of longing go through her before she could stop it.

Where had that illicit fantasy come from? One of the reasons she'd agreed to marry Rio—apart from her concern for the boys—was because after years of being an outsider in other people's homes as a foster child it had been easier to contemplate a marriage of convenience than to dare dream that she might one day have a real family of her own…

The prospect of Cruz ever seeing that deeply inside her made her go clammy all over.

Her arms tightened. 'I'm not going out this evening because I think the boys are coming down with something and I want to observe them for twenty-four hours to make sure they're okay. Sancho still isn't over his bug completely.'

Cruz glanced at the boys and back to her. 'They look fine to me.'

'They were off their food at breakfast, which isn't like them.'

'Mrs Jordan can watch them, and call us if she's worried.'

Exasperated, Trinity unfolded her arms and put her hands on her hips. 'You don't get it, do you? I'm worried about them, and even if it's only a niggle then I will put them first. *I* am the one they need if they're not feeling well.'

Scathingly, Cruz said, 'So you're not above using my nephews as an excuse?'

Hurt that he should think her capable of such a thing she said, 'Their welfare comes first, so I don't really care what you think.'

Cruz's jaw clenched, and then he just said, 'Seven p.m., Trinity. Be ready.' And then he turned and walked away.

To her shame she couldn't stop her gaze from dropping down his broad back to where his worn jeans showed off his powerful buttocks. Disgusted with herself, she whirled around and went over to the boys who, she had to admit, would look fine to most observers but not to her, who knew all their little habits and foibles.

Something wasn't quite right and she wasn't going to let Cruz bully her.

Later that evening Cruz's blood was boiling. No one had ever stood him up. Certainly not a woman. But Trinity had. Julia, looking terrified—*was he really that scary?*—had come with a note when he'd been waiting for Trinity in the hall.

Sorry, Cruz, but I'm just not certain the boys aren't coming down with something. I'm not coming. T.

The note was crumpled in his palm now, as he strode along the dark corridors to the wing Trinity and the boys occupied. Something about the oppressiveness of the *castillo* scraped along his nerves, when it never really had before. It was as if having Trinity and the boys here was throwing everything into sharp relief...

When he was near the boys' bedroom he could hear fractious cries and Trinity's tones, soothing. He stopped in the doorway to see her changing a clearly cranky Sancho into his pyjamas.

Mateo was running around in his nappy. As soon as he saw Cruz he sped over. 'Come play, Unkel Cooz!'

Cruz's chest felt tight. He bent down. 'Not now, *chiquito*. Tomorrow.'

He put his hand to Mateo's head and it felt warm. He looked up to see Trinity standing in front of him, still wearing the jeans and shirt she'd had on earlier. She really wasn't coming.

He straightened up and a determined expression came over her face. 'I meant it, Cruz, I'm worried about the boys. They've been off their food all day and they're both running slight temperatures. They also didn't nap today, so they're overtired now. It's probably nothing serious, but I'm not leaving them. I've given Mrs Jordan the evening off so she can take over in the morning.'

Cruz was slightly stunned yet again to think that she wasn't even their mother. Right now, with the boys in the room behind her, he had the distinct impression of a mother bear guarding her cubs from danger. He couldn't figure out what she could possibly be gaining from this if she *was* playing some game.

To his surprise something dark gripped his gut, and it took him a moment to acknowledge uncomfortably that it was jealousy—and something else...something more ambiguous that went deeper.

Jealousy of his nephews, who were being afforded such care and protection—the kind of protection he'd vowed to give them but which now he realised he was too woefully inexperienced to give.

The something deeper was a sharp sense of poignancy that his own mother had never cared for him like this. *Dios*, even his nanny hadn't shown this much concern.

Feeling very uncharacteristically at a momentary loss, he recognised that for the first time in his life he would have to back down.

'Call me if they get worse, or if you need anything. Maria the housekeeper has the number of my doctor.'

Trinity nodded, shocked that Cruz was conceding. She'd half expected him to insist on dressing her himself and dragging her out of the *castillo*.

He stepped away and said, 'I'll check on you when I get back.'

The thought of him coming in later, with his bow tie undone and looking far too sexy, made her say quickly, 'There's no—'

He looked at her warningly. 'I'll check on you.'

'Okay.'

For a moment something seemed to shimmer between them—something fragile. Then Cruz turned and left and she breathed out an unsteady breath. She turned around to focus on the boys and told herself that she'd just been imagining that moment of softening between them. Wishful thinking.

When Cruz returned later that night he went straight to the boys' room, where a low light leaked from under the door. He ruminated that he hadn't enjoyed one minute of the function—not that he usually did, because he considered these events work—and he realised now with some irritation that he'd missed having Trinity at his side. Seeing her reaction to everything. Having her close enough to touch.

He opened the door softly and stepped in. His eyes immediately tracked to the two small figures in their beds and he went over, finding himself pulling their covers back over their bodies from where they'd kicked them off. Something turned over in his chest at seeing them sprawled across their beds, dark lashes long on plump cheeks, hair tousled. They looked so innocent, defenceless. Once again he was overcome with a sense of protectiveness.

Then he looked up and saw another figure, curled in the armchair near the beds. Trinity. She was asleep, her head resting on her shoulder. A book lay open on her thigh and he looked at it: *The A-Z of Toddlers*.

For a moment he felt blindsided at this evidence of her dedication. That sense of poignancy he'd felt earlier gripped him again, and it was deeply disturbing and exposing.

Something else prickled under his skin now. If she was playing a game then it was a very elaborate one.

He recalled her coming into his office last night and her words: *'All that stuff that Rio told you about me being a gold-digger...none of it is true.'*

Cruz's rational mind reminded him that there was evidence of her treachery. Her name on receipts. Demands she'd made. Rio's humiliation. Maybe this was her game— she was trying to convince him she was something she wasn't and would wriggle under his skin like she had with Rio until he too felt compelled to give her everything...

'Cruz?'

She was awake now, blinking up at him. She sat up, looking deliciously dishevelled, compounding the myriad conflicting emotions she evoked.

His voice was gruff when he spoke. 'Go to bed, Trinity. I'll sit up with them.'

She looked flustered. 'No!' She lowered her voice. 'You don't have to do that. It's fine… I think they're okay now, anyway. Their temperatures were normal last time I checked.'

'Go to bed. I'll let you know if anything happens.'

She looked up at him helplessly and he offered ruefully, 'I'm going to have to get used to doing this kind of thing. I'm their uncle, and I don't intend to treat them like guests in my home.'

For the first time since Rio had died it struck Cruz forcibly that he hadn't really thought about how taking responsibility for his nephews would affect him until now. And this was what it meant, he realised with a kind of belated wonder. Being concerned. Sitting up all night to watch over them if need be.

Trinity eyes were wide, and even in this light Cruz could see the smudges of fatigue under them. From this angle he could also see down her shirt to the bountiful swells of her breasts. His body reacted.

He gritted out, 'Just go.'

She stood up jerkily, as if her muscles were protesting. 'You'll let me know if they wake?' She sounded uncertain.

Cruz nodded and took her place on the chair, stretching out his long legs and picking up the book. He gestured with it for her to go.

Feeling more than a little discombobulated at having woken to find Cruz standing over her, looking exactly like the sexy fantasy she'd envisaged earlier, Trinity eventually moved towards her own room, glancing back to see Cruz tipping his head back and closing his eyes, hands linked loosely across his flat abdomen.

Her footsteps faltered, though, as she was momentarily transfixed by the fact that he had insisted on staying. Emotion expanded in her chest at the domestic scene—dangerous emotion—as she thought how incongruous he looked here, yet how *right*.

His willingness to forge a bond with his nephews made that emotion turn awfully poignant… She had a vision of going over to him, smoothing his hair back…of him looking up at her and reaching for her, smiling sexily as he pulled her down onto his lap…

Shock at the vividness of this fantasy made her breathless. And at how much she yearned for it. When it was only his nephews he cared about. Not her.

Without opening his eyes, Cruz said softly, 'Go to bed, Trinity.'

And she fled before he might see any vestige of that momentary fantasy on her face.

When Trinity woke the following morning it was later than she'd ever slept since she'd started looking after the twins. And they were her first thought.

She shot out of bed and went into their room, to see that their beds were empty and their pyjamas were neatly folded on their pillows.

She washed quickly and got dressed in jeans and a T-shirt, pulling her hair back into a low ponytail as she went down to the dining room, where she found Mrs Jordan and the twins.

'*Mummy!*' they both screeched in unison when they saw her, and her heart swelled.

She went over and kissed them both. She looked at the older woman. 'You should have woken me.'

Mrs Jordan waved a hand. 'Cruz wouldn't hear of it. He insisted that you sleep in and I agreed. You've been looking tired lately.'

Trinity's heart skipped. She still felt raw after that moment of insanity when she'd wished for a domestic idyll that would never exist.

'He was still there this morning?'

She sat down and helped herself to coffee, noting with relief that the boys seemed to be making up for their lack of appetite the previous day, with their mouths full of mushy cereal.

Mrs Jordan nodded and a look of unmistakable awe came over her face. 'He was changing them when I went in this morning, and apart from putting Sancho's nappy on back to front he didn't do a bad job at all...'

Trinity choked on her coffee, spraying some out of her mouth inelegantly, and the boys went into paroxysms of giggles.

'Funny, Mummy...do it again!'

She distracted them for a minute, playing aeroplanes with their spoons as she fed them, and avoided Mrs Jordan's far too shrewd gaze. She almost felt angry with Cruz for blurring the boundaries like this and inducing disturbing fantasies. And then she felt awful—she should be happy that he was intent on connecting with his nephews in a real and meaningful way.

After the boys had finished their breakfast, and Mrs Jordan had taken them outside to play, Trinity sipped her coffee, recalling again how dangerously intimate it had felt to share that space with Cruz last night. And how seductive.

Just then a sound made her look up and her heart stopped at the sight of the object of her thoughts standing in the doorway, dressed in a three-piece suit, looking so gorgeous it hurt.

He came in and Trinity still felt a little raw, unprepared to see him. It made her voice stiff. 'Thank you for watching the boys last night.'

Cruz poured himself a cup of coffee and took a seat opposite her. He shook his head minutely. 'Like I said, I'm going to be in their lives in a meaningful way.'

Feeling absurdly shy, she said, 'Mrs Jordan told me you changed them.'

Cruz's eyes gleamed with wry humour and it took Trinity's breath away. 'I won't ever again underestimate the ability of a two-and-a-half-year-old to create a toxic smell to rival the effluent of a chemical plant. Or the skill it takes to change one of those things.'

Cruz took a sip of his coffee and put down the cup. 'I've arranged for some potential nannies to come later today, for you and Mrs Jordan to interview.'

'Do you really think that's necessary?'

'Yes.' The wry gleam was gone from his eyes now. 'I've been invited to an event at the newly refurbished opera house in Madrid this Friday night, and I have meetings to attend in the afternoon. Barring any unforeseen events, I am asking you to attend the function with me in Madrid. We'll be gone until Saturday. It'll be a good opportunity for the new nanny to start and get used to the boys under Mrs Jordan's supervision.'

Two things were bombarding Trinity at once. Namely he fact that he was *asking* her, even if it was slightly mocking, and that she'd be away for a whole night with Cruz.

'But I've never left the boys for that long before.'

His tone was dry. 'I think they'll survive less than twenty-four hours without you, and with two nannies in attendance. I spoke with Mrs Jordan about it earlier—she's fine.'

Of course she was, thought Trinity churlishly. Mrs Jordan was his number one fan.

'Tell me, Trinity,' Cruz asked silkily, 'is the reason you're reluctant because you fear maintaining the lie that you don't want me? Are you afraid that you won't be able to control your urges if we're alone? I don't think it's out of concern for the boys at all—I think it's much more personal.'

She felt shamed. He was right. She *was* scared—scared of her reactions around this man. Scared of what might happen if he touched her again. Scared to have him see underneath to where her real vulnerabilities lay. Scared of what he would do if he were faced with the ultimate truth of just how deeply Rio had loathed him. Her guts twisted at the thought in a way that told her she was far more invested in this man than she liked to admit.

But as Cruz looked at her, waiting for her response, she knew she couldn't keep running. She could resist him. She had to.

Coolly she ignored what he'd said and replied, 'Friday should be fine. What time do we leave?'

A few days later Trinity risked looking at Cruz from where she sat in the back of the chauffeur-driven limousine that had picked them up at Madrid airport, but he was engrossed in his palm tablet on the other side of the car, seemingly oblivious to her. She'd just had a conversation on her mobile phone with Mrs Jordan, to check on her and the boys and the new nanny, who were all fine.

As if reading her mind, Cruz put down his tablet and looked at her, that golden amber gaze sweeping down her body and taking in the very elegant and classic sheath dress and matching jacket she'd put on that day in a bid to look presentable.

His gaze narrowed on her assessingly, and she had to fight not to squirm self-consciously. 'What is it?'

She was half raising a hand to check her hair when Cruz answered simply, 'You're a good mother to them.'

If there'd been a grudging tone in his voice Trinity would have hated him, but there hadn't. He'd sounded… reluctantly impressed. She desperately tried to ignore the rush of warmth inside her that signified how much she wanted his approval.

'I love them, Cruz, even though they're not mine.' Impulsively she asked, 'Why is that so hard for you to believe? Is it because of your upbringing?'

He smiled, but it wasn't a nice smile. 'You could say that. Rio wasn't the only one neglected in the *castillo*. Once she'd had me, my mother considered her maternal duty taken care of. She didn't love me, and she didn't love my father either. Their marriage was a purely strategic one, bringing two powerful families together as was the tradition in my family for centuries.'

Cruz's eyeline shifted over Trinity's shoulder just as the car came to a smooth halt on a wide tree-lined street.

'We're here,' he said, leaving Trinity's brain buzzing with what he'd just shared.

She looked out of the window on her side, saw a scrum of men with cameras waiting for them and instantly felt nervous. She'd always hated the way Rio had wanted to court as much media attention as possible.

Cruz said tersely, 'Wait in the car. I'll come round to get you.'

Trinity would have been quite happy if the car had turned around and taken them straight back to the airport.

When Cruz appeared outside the car the scrum had become a sea of flashing lights and shouting. Her door was opened and his hand reached in for her. She took it like a lifeline. He hustled her into the foyer of the gleaming building and within seconds they were in the elevator and ascending with a soft *whoosh*.

It was the hushed silence after the cacophony of sound that registered first, and then Trinity became burningly aware that she was pressed from thigh to breast into Cruz's body. His free arm was around her shoulder and her other hand was still in his, held over his taut belly.

She couldn't be any closer to him if she climbed into his very skin.

She scrambled apart from him, dislodging his arm and taking her hand from his. She couldn't look at him. For a split second before she'd come to her senses she'd loved the sensation of his strength surrounding her, and for someone who'd long ago learnt to depend on herself it was scary how easy it had felt just to…give in.

Thankfully the lift doors opened at that moment, and the sight that greeted Trinity took her breath away. She stepped out into a huge open space dominated on all sides by massive glass windows which showcased the breath-taking view of one of Europe's most beautiful and stately cities.

She walked over to one of the windows and could see a huge cathedral soaring into the blue sky.

'That's the Almudena Cathedral, infamous for taking five hundred years to complete.'

Cruz's voice was far too close, but Trinity fought the urge to move away and instead turned around to take in the penthouse apartment. It was unmistakably a bachelor pad, every inch of every surface gleaming and pristine. But it was also cultured—low tables held massive coffee table books on photography and art. Bookshelves lined one entire interior wall. Huge modern art canvases sat in the centre of the few walls not showcasing the view.

'Let me show you around.'

Trinity followed Cruz as he guided her through a stunning modern kitchen that led into a formal dining room, and then to where a series of rooms off a long corridor revealed themselves to be sumptuous en-suite bedrooms and an office.

When they were back in the main open-plan living and dining area, she felt a little dazed. 'Your apartment is stunning.'

'But not exactly toddler-proof.'

She looked at Cruz, surprised that he'd articulated the

very thing she'd just been thinking in her head: it was beautiful apartment but a potential death trap for small energetic boys.

He glanced at her and she quickly closed her open mouth, looking around again. 'No. Not exactly.'

'I will ensure this place is made child-friendly for when the boys come to visit. I intend on my nephews becoming familiar with their capital city. This is where the seat of the main De Carrillo bank has been since the Middle Ages. This is where their legacy resides, as much as it does in Seville.'

Their capital city. It had been said with such effortless arrogance. But the truth was that Cruz was right—he was undoubtedly a titan of this city. Probably owned a huge swathe of it. And the twins would one day inherit all this.

It was mind-boggling to contemplate, and for the first time Trinity felt a sense of fear for the boys and this huge responsibility they'd have one day.

She rounded on Cruz. 'What happens if Matty and Sancho don't want any of this?'

His gaze narrowed on her and something flashed across his face before she could decipher it. Something almost pained.

'Believe me, I will do what's best for my nephews. They will not be forced to take on anything they can't handle or don't want. I won't let that happen to them.'

Trinity's anger deflated. She'd heard the emotion in Cruz's voice. Almost as if he was referring to someone who *had* taken on something they couldn't handle. Was he thinking of Rio and the irresponsible and lavish way he'd lived?

Cruz looked at his watch. 'I have to go to meetings now, but I'll be back to get ready for the function this evening. We'll leave at six p.m.'

Before he left he took something out of his inner pocket. He handed her a black credit card.

She took it warily. 'What is this? A test?'

His face was unreadable, but she wasn't fooled. She knew he'd be assessing her every reaction.

'You'll need access to funds. Do what you want for the afternoon—a driver will be at your disposal downstairs.'

He left then, and for a long minute Trinity found herself wondering if he *had* been talking about Rio not being able to handle things...

Then, disgusted with herself for obsessing like this, she threw the credit card down on a nearby table and paced over to a window. When she looked down to the street far below she could see Cruz disappearing into the back of another sleek Jeep.

It pulled into the flow of traffic and she shivered slightly, as if he could somehow still see her. He was so all-encompassing that it was hard to believe he wasn't omnipresent.

She sighed and leaned forward, placing her hot forehead against the cool glass. It felt as if every time they took a step forward they then took three backwards. Clearly the credit card was some kind of a test, and he expected her to revert to type when given half a chance.

Cruz was standing with his back to the recently emptied boardroom on the top floor of the De Carrillo bank, loosening his tie and opening a top button on his shirt. Madrid was laid out before him, with the lowering sun leaving long shadows over the streets below where people were leaving their offices.

He hated himself for it, but as soon as the last person had left the room he'd pulled out his phone to make a call, too impatient to wait.

'*Where* did she go?' he asked incredulously, his hand dropping from his shirt.

His driver answered. 'She went to the Plaza Mayor, where she had a coffee, and then she spent the afternoon in the Museo Del Prado. She's just returned to the apartment.'

'And she walked,' Cruz repeated flatly, not liking the way the thought of her sightseeing around Madrid on her own made him feel a twinge of conscience. As if he'd neglected her. 'No shopping?'

'No, sir, apart from two cuddly toys in the museum shop.'

Cruz terminated the call. So Trinity hadn't spent the day shopping in Calle de Serrano, home to the most lavish boutiques. He had to admit that the credit card *had* been a test, and a pretty crude one at that. But once again either she was playing a longer game than he'd given her credit for…or he had to acknowledge that she had changed. Fundamentally. And in Cruz's experience of human nature that just wasn't possible.

Cruz didn't deal in unknowns. It was one of the driving motives behind his marrying Trinity—to make sure she was kept very much within his sphere of *knowns*.

Suddenly he wasn't so sure of anything any more.

But *how* could he trust her over his own brother?

He could still see the humiliation on Rio's face when he'd had to explain to Cruz that that his own wife had tipped him over the edge. Cruz knew that Rio's lavish lifestyle and his first wife had undoubtedly started the process of his ultimate destruction, but Trinity had finished it off. And, worse, used his nephews to gain privileged access.

But then he thought of her, standing between him and his nephews the other night, so adamant that they came first. And he thought of how he'd found her, curled up asleep in the chair… He shook his head angrily and turned away from the window. *Merda*, she was messing with his head.

Cruz blocked out the niggles of his conscience. He would be the biggest fool on earth if he was to believe in this newly minted Trinity De Carrillo without further evidence. She was playing a game—she had to be. It was that simple. And he had no choice but to go along with it for now…

Because eventually she would reveal her true self, and when she did Cruz would be waiting.

CHAPTER SEVEN

A COUPLE OF hours later Cruz's mind was no less tangled. The woman beside him was drawing every single eye in the extravagantly designed and decorated open-air court-yard of the new opera house. When he'd arrived back at the apartment she'd been in her room getting ready, so he'd been showered and changed before he'd seen her, waiting for him in the living area of the apartment.

The shock of that first glimpse of her still ran through his system, constricting his breath and pumping blood to tender places. She wore a strapless black dress that was moulded to every curve. Over one shoulder was a sliver of chiffon tied in a bow.

She wore no jewellery apart from the engagement ring and her wedding band. Her nails were unpainted. Minimal make-up. And yet people couldn't stop looking at her. *He* couldn't stop looking at her.

Very uncharacteristically, Cruz wanted to snarl at them all to look at their own partners. But he couldn't, because he could see what they saw—a glowing diamond amidst the dross. She appealed to this jaded crowd because she had an unfashionable air of wonder about her as she looked around, which only reinforced the shadow of doubt in his mind…

Just then her arm tightened in his and he looked down to see a flush on her cheeks. She was biting her lip. Irritated at the effect she had on him, he said more curtly than he'd intended, 'What is it?'

She sounded hesitant. 'I shouldn't have put my hair up like this. I look ridiculous.'

Cruz looked at her hair, which was in a sleek high ponytail. He didn't consider himself an expert on women's hair-styles, but he could see that the other women had more complicated things going on. Another reason why Trinity stood out so effortlessly. She looked unfussy—simple and yet sexy as sin all at once.

'Someone left a fashion magazine on the table in the café earlier and I saw pictures of models with their hair up like this. I thought it was a thing...'

The shadow of doubt loomed larger. He thought of how she'd shrunk back from the paparazzi earlier. She certainly hadn't been flaunting herself, looking for attention. Anything but. She'd clung to him as if terrified.

He took her arm above the elbow and she looked up at him. He could see the uncertainty and embarrassment in her eyes. It was getting harder and harder to see her as the cold-hearted mercenary gold-digger who had willingly fleeced his brother.

His voice was gruff. 'Your hair is absolutely fine. They're looking because you're the most beautiful woman here.'

Trinity was disorientated by Cruz's compliment. He'd barely said two words to her since he'd got back to the apartment and they'd left to go out again, and he'd just looked at her suspiciously when he'd asked her what she'd done for the afternoon.

Cruz was staring at her now, in a way that made her heart thump unevenly. But then a low, melodic gong sounded, breaking the weird moment.

He looked away from her and up. 'It's time for the banquet.'

Breathing a sigh of relief at being released from that intensity, and not really sure what it meant, she followed Cruz into a huge ballroom that had the longest dining table she'd ever seen in her life. Opulent flowers overflowed from vases and twined all along the table in artful disarray. A thousand candles flickered, and low lights glinted off the solid gold cutlery. She sighed in pure wonder at the scene—it was like a movie set.

And then she spotted Lexie Anderson, the famous actress, and her gorgeous husband, Cesar Da Silva, and felt as if she'd really been transported into a movie. The stunning petite blonde and her tall husband were completely engrossed in each other, and it made something poignant ache inside her.

'Trinity?'

She blushed, hating it that Cruz might have caught her staring at the other couple, and sat down in the chair he was holding out for her.

When she was seated, Trinity saw Cruz walking away and she whispered after him. 'Wait, where are you going?'

He stopped. 'I've been seated opposite you—beside the president of the Spanish Central Bank.'

'Oh, okay.' Trinity feigned nonchalance, even though she was taking in the vast size of the table and realising he might as well be sitting in another room.

Of course he couldn't resist the opportunity to mock her. He came back and bent down, saying close to her ear, 'Don't tell me you'll miss me, *querida*?'

'Don't be ridiculous,' she snapped, angry that she'd shown how gauche she was. She turned away, but hated it that her stomach lurched at the thought of being left alone to fend for herself in an environment where she'd never felt comfortable.

She couldn't take her eyes off him as he walked around to the other side of the table, being stopped and adored by several people on his way. One of them was Cesar Da Silva, who got up to shake Cruz's hand, and the two tall and ridiculously handsome men drew lots of lingering looks. He even bent down to kiss Lexie Anderson on both cheeks, and it caused a funny twisting sensation in Trinity's stomach, seeing him bestow affection so easily on anyone but her.

No, what he'd bestow on *her* was much darker and full of anger and mistrust.

Determined not to be intimidated, Trinity tried talking to the person on her left, but he couldn't speak English and she had no Spanish so that went nowhere. She had more luck with an attractive older gentleman on her right, who turned out to be a diplomat and did speak English, and who put her at ease as only a diplomat could.

Finally she felt herself relax for the first time in weeks, chuckling at her companion's funny stories of various diplomatic disasters. With Cruz on the other side of the very large and lavishly decorated table she relished a reprieve from the constant tension she felt around him, even if she fancied she could feel his golden gaze boring into her through the elaborate foliage. She resisted the urge to look in his direction. She'd already given far too much away.

After the coffee cups had been cleared away her dinner partner's attention was taken by the person on his other side. Trinity risked a look across the table and saw that Cruz's seat was empty. And then she spotted him—because it would be impossible to miss him. He was walking towards her with that lean animal grace, eyes narrowed on her, this time oblivious to people's attempts to get his attention.

The tension was back instantly. Making her feel tingly and alive as much as wary. When he reached her he didn't even have to touch her for a shiver to run through her body.

'Cold?' The tone of his voice was innocuous, but the expression on his face was hard.

Trinity shook her head, feeling a sense of vertigo as she looked up, even though she was sitting down. 'No, not cold.'

'Enjoying yourself?'

Now his words had definite bite in them, and she saw his eyeline shift over her head. 'Nice to see you, Lopez,' he drawled. 'Thank you for keeping my wife amused.'

The man's smoothly cultured voice floated over Trinity's shoulder.

'The pleasure was all mine, De Carrillo. Trinity is a charming, beautiful woman. A breath of fresh air.'

Trinity watched, fascinated, as Cruz's face darkened and a muscle ticked in his jaw. 'Then I'm sorry that I must deprive you of her presence. I believe the dancing has started.'

She barely had time to get a word out to say goodbye to the other man before Cruz was all but hauling her out of her chair and onto the dance floor, where a band was playing slow, sexy jazz songs. His arm was like steel around her back and her other hand was clasped in his, high against his chest.

He moved around the floor with such effortless expertise that Trinity didn't have time to worry about her two left feet. To her horror, though, she felt absurdly vulnerable, reminded of how lonely she'd felt during the day even while she'd appreciated the beautiful majesty of Madrid.

She'd missed Matty and Sancho and she'd felt a very rare surge of self-pity, wondering if this would be her life now—forever on the periphery of Cruz's antipathy.

It was a long time since she'd indulged in such a weak emotion and it made her voice sharp. 'What do you think you're doing?'

Cruz's mouth was a thin line. 'I'm not sure. Maybe you want to tell me? Sebastian Lopez is a millionaire and renowned for his penchant for beautiful young women—maybe you knew that and saw an opportunity to seek a more benevolent benefactor?'

Trinity fought to control her breathing and her temper, and hated it that she was so aware of every inch of her body, which seemed to be welded against his.

'Don't be ridiculous,' she hissed. 'He's old enough to be my father and there was nothing remotely flirtatious about our conversation.' She tilted her head back as much as she could so she could look Cruz dead in the eye. 'But do you know what? It was nice to talk to someone who doesn't think I'm one step above a common thief.'

Terrified that Cruz would see emotion she shouldn't be feeling, she managed to pull herself out of his embrace and stalked off the dance floor, apologising as she bumped into another couple. She walked blindly, half expecting a heavy hand on her shoulder at any moment, but of course Cruz wouldn't appreciate that public display of discord.

She made it out to the marbled foyer area, where a few people milled around, and walked out to the entrance. She sucked in a breath to try and steady her heart. Night was enfolding Madrid in a glorious velvet glow but it couldn't soothe her ragged nerves.

It wasn't long before she felt Cruz's presence. The little hairs all over her body seemed to stand up and quiver in his direction. She refused to feel foolish for storming off. He'd insulted her.

He came to stand beside her, but said nothing as his car arrived at the front of the building with a soft sleek purr. Trinity cursed the fact that she hadn't been quicker to call a cab. Cruz held open the back door and she avoided his eye as she got in, not wanting to see the undoubtedly volcanic expression on his face.

As the driver pulled into the light evening traffic Trinity said frigidly, 'You don't have to leave. You should stay. Your brother soon learned that it made more sense to let me leave early.'

* * *

Cruz was in the act of yanking at his bow tie and opening his top button, wanting to feel less constricted. But now his hand stilled and the red haze of anger that had descended over his vision during the course of the evening as he'd watched Trinity talking and laughing with that man finally started to dissipate.

'What did you just say?' he asked.

Trinity was staring straight ahead, her profile perfect. But she was tense—her full lips pursed, jaw rigid.

It slammed into him then—the truth he'd been trying to deny. He was insanely jealous. He'd been jealous since the day she'd walked out of his house and got into Rio's car to go and work for him.

At that moment she looked at him, and he could feel himself tipping over the edge of an abyss. Those huge blue eyes were full of such...*injury*.

Her voice was tight. 'I said that your brother soon learned that I don't fit into those events well. I'm not from that world, and I don't know what to do or say.'

She clamped her mouth shut then, as if she'd said enough already.

Cruz reeled. His impression had been that Rio had taken her everywhere and that she'd loved it and milked it, but something in the tightness of her voice told him she wasn't lying, and that revelation only added to the doubts clamouring for attention in his head.

He tried and failed to block out the fact that when she'd pulled free of his arms on the dance floor and stalked away he'd thought he'd seen the glitter of tears in her eyes.

She turned her head away again and he saw the column of her throat working. His gaze took in an expanse of pale skin, slim shoulders, delicate clavicle, the enticing curve of her breasts under the material of the dress, and heat engulfed him along with something much more nebulous:

an urge to comfort, which was as bewildering as it was impossible to resist.

He reached across and touched Trinity's chin, turning her face towards him again. 'I'm sorry,' he said. 'You didn't deserve that. The truth is that I didn't like seeing you with that man.'

The shock on her face might have insulted Cruz if he hadn't been so distracted by those huge eyes.

Her mouth opened and the tense line of her jaw relaxed slightly. 'I...okay. Apology accepted.'

That simple. Another woman would have made the most of Cruz's uncharacteristic apology.

His thumb moved back and forth across Trinity's jaw, the softness of her delicate skin an enticement to touch and keep touching.

'What are you doing?'

He dragged his gaze up over high cheekbones, perfect bone structure. 'I can't *not* touch you.' The admission seemed to fall out of him before he could stop it.

Trinity put a hand up over his. The car came to a smooth stop. Cruz knew that he had to keep touching her or die. And he assured himself that it had nothing to do with the emotion that had clouded his judgement and his vision as he'd watched her at ease with another man, and everything to do with pure, unadulterated lust.

Trinity was locked into Cruz's eyes and the intensity of his gaze. One minute she'd been hurt and angry, and then he'd apologised...once again demonstrating a level of humility that she just wouldn't have expected from him. And now... Now she was burning up under his explicit look that told her that whatever they'd just been talking about was forgotten, that things had taken a far more carnal turn.

She felt a breeze touch her back. She blinked and looked

around to see the driver standing at the door, waiting for her to get out. They'd arrived back at the apartment building and she hadn't even noticed.

She scrambled out inelegantly, feeling seriously jittery. It was as if some kind of silent communication had passed between them, and she wasn't sure what she'd agreed to.

The journey up to the apartment passed in a blur. The lift doors opened and they stepped into the hushed interior of Cruz's apartment. He threw off his jacket and Trinity's mouth dried as she watched the play of muscles under the thin silk of his shirt.

He glanced back at her over his shoulder. 'I know you don't really drink, but would you like something?'

Trinity was about to refuse, but something in the air made her feel uncharacteristically reckless. She moved forward. 'Okay.'

'What would you like?'

She stopped, her mind a blank. Embarrassment engulfed her—she was no sophisticate.

Cruz looked at her. 'I've got all the spirits. What do you like?'

Trinity shrugged one shoulder. 'I'm not sure…'

He looked at her for a long moment and then turned back to the drinks table, doing something she couldn't see. Then he turned and came towards her with two glasses. One was large and bulbous, filled with what looked like brandy or whisky. The other glass was smaller, with an orange liquid over a couple of ice cubes.

He handed her the second glass. 'Try this—see what you think.'

After a moment's hesitation she reached for the glass and bent her head, taking a sniff. Cruz was waiting for her reaction, so she took a sip of the cool liquid and it slid down her throat, leaving a sweet aftertaste. She wrinkled her nose, because she'd been expecting something tart or strong.

She looked at him. 'It's sweet. I like it—what is it?'

A small smile played around the corner of Cruz's mouth. 'It's Pacharán—a Spanish liqueur from Navarre. Very distinctive. It tastes sweet, but it packs quite the alcoholic punch. Hence the small amount.'

Before he could suck her under and scramble her brain cells with just a look Trinity went and sat down at the end of one couch, bemused by this very fragile cessation in hostilities. Cruz sat too, choosing the end of a couch at right angles to hers. He effortlessly filled the space with his muscled bulk, long legs stretched out, almost touching hers.

Trinity felt unaccountably nervous, and a little bewildered. She was so used to Cruz coming at her with his judgement and mistrust that she wasn't sure how to navigate these waters. He sat forward, hands loose around his glass, drawing her attention to long fingers.

'Tell me something about yourself—like your name. How did you get it?'

She tensed all over. Every instinct within her was screaming to resist this far more dangerous Cruz. 'What are you doing? You're not interested in who I am...you don't have to ask me these things.'

'You were the one,' he pointed out reasonably, 'who said we need to learn to get along.'

And look how that had ended up—with him kissing her and demonstrating just how weak she was. What could she say, though? He was right.

Hating it that she was exposing her agitation, but needing space from his focus on her, Trinity stood up and walked over to one of the windows, holding her glass to her chest like some kind of ineffectual armour.

Looking out at the view, she said as lightly as she could,

'I was called Trinity after the church where I was found abandoned on the steps. The Holy Trinity Church in Islington.'

She heard movement and sensed Cruz coming to stand near her. She could feel his eyes on her.

'Go on,' he said.

Night had descended over Madrid, and the skyline was lit up spectacularly against the inky blackness.

'They think I was just a few hours old, but they can't be sure, and it wasn't long after midnight, so they nominated that date as my birthday. I was wrapped in a blanket. The priest found me.'

'What happened then?'

Trinity swallowed. 'The authorities waited as long as they could for my biological parent, or parents, to come and claim me. By the time I was a toddler I was in foster care, and there was still no sign of anyone claiming me, so they put me forward for adoption.'

'But your file said you grew up in foster homes.'

Trinity was still astounded that he'd looked into her past. She glanced at him, but looked away again quickly. 'I did grow up in foster homes. But I was adopted for about a year, until the couple's marriage broke up and they decided they didn't want to keep me if they weren't staying together.'

She shouldn't be feeling emotion—not after all these years. But it was still there…the raw, jagged edges of hurt at the knowledge that she'd been abandoned by her own mother and then hadn't even managed to persuade her adoptive parents to keep her.

'Apparently,' she said, as dispassionately as she could, 'I was traumatised, so they decided it might be best not to put me through that experience again. That's how I ended up in the foster home system.'

'Were you moved around much?'

'Not at the start. But when I came into my teens, yes. I was in about six different foster homes before I turned eighteen.'

'Your affinity with Mateo and Sancho… You have no qualification in childcare, and yet you obviously know what to do with small children.'

Trinity felt as if Cruz was peeling back layers of skin. It was almost physically painful to talk about this. 'For some reason the small children in the foster homes used to latch on to me… I felt protective, and I liked mothering them, watching over them…'

But then the inevitable always happened—the babies and toddlers would be taken away to another home, or put up for adoption, and Trinity would be bereft. And yet each time it had happened she'd been helpless to resist the instinct to nurture. Of course, she surmised grimly now, a psychologist would undoubtedly tell her she'd been desperately trying to fulfil the need in herself to be loved and cared for.

And the twins were evidence that she hadn't learned to fill that gap on her own yet.

'Did you ever go looking for your parents?'

Trinity fought to control her emotions. 'Where would I start? It wasn't as if they'd logged their names anywhere. I could have investigated pregnant women on record in the local area, who had never returned to give birth, but to be honest I decided a long time ago that perhaps it was best to just leave it alone.'

The truth was that she didn't think she could survive the inevitable rejection of her parents if she ever found either one of them.

She felt her glass being lifted out of her hands, and looked to see Cruz putting it down on a side table beside his. He turned back and took her hand in his, turning it

over, looking at it as if it held some answer he was looking for. The air between them was charged.

'What are you doing?' Trinity asked shakily.

Their eyes met and she desperately wanted to move
back, out of Cruz's magnetic orbit, but she couldn't.

'You're an enigma,' he said, meeting her eyes. 'I can't
figure you out and it bothers me.'

Feeling even shakier now, she said, 'There's nothing to
figure out. What you see is what you get.'

Cruz gripped her hand tighter and pulled her closer, saying gruffly, 'I'm beginning to wonder if that isn't the case.'

It took a second for his words to sink in, and when they
did Trinity's belly went into freefall. Was he…could he really listen to her now? And believe her?

But Cruz didn't seem to be interested in talking. His
hand was trailing up her arm now, all the way to where
the chiffon was tied at her shoulder.

With slow, sure movements, and not taking his eyes off
hers, Cruz undid the bow, letting the material fall down.
He caressed her shoulder, moving his hand around to the
back of her neck and then up, finding the band in her hair
and tugging it free so that her hair fell down around her
shoulders.

Trinity was feeling incredibly vulnerable after revealing far more than she'd intended, but Cruz was looking at
her and touching her as if he was burning up inside, just
as she was, making her forget everything. Almost.

She couldn't let him expose her even more…

It was the hardest thing in the world, but she caught his
hand, pulling it away. 'We shouldn't do this…'

He turned her hand in his, so he was holding it again,
pulling her even closer so she could feel every inch of her
body against his much harder one.

'Oh, yes, we should, *querida*. It's inevitable. The truth
is that it's been inevitable since we first kissed.'

Cruz wrapped both hands around her upper arms. Trinity's world was reduced down to the beats of her heart and the heat prickling all over her skin. Surely his mention of that cataclysmic night should be breaking them out of this spell? But it wasn't…

A dangerous lassitude seeped into her blood, draining her will to resist. Cruz bent his head close to hers, his breath feathering over her mouth.

'Tell me you want this, Trinity. At least this is true between us—you can't deny it.'

She was in a very dangerous place—feeling exposed after her confession and the tantalising suggestion that Cruz might be prepared to admit that he was wrong about her… All her defences were snapping and falling to pieces.

As if sensing her inner vacillation, Cruz touched her bare shoulder with his mouth and moved up to where her neck met her shoulder. He whispered against her skin. 'Tell me…'

Unable to stop herself, she heard the words falling out of her mouth. 'I want you…'

He pulled back, a fierce expression on his face. Triumph. It made her dizzy. She didn't even have time to think of the repercussions before Cruz's mouth was on hers and suddenly everything was slotting into place. She didn't have to think…she only had to feel. It was heady, and too seductive to resist.

The intimacy of his tongue stroking roughly along hers made blood pool between her legs, hot and urgent. Pulsing in time with her heart.

Time slowed down as Cruz stole her very soul right out from inside her. A fire was taking root and incinerating everything in its path.

His hands landed on her waist, hauling her right into him, where she could feel the solid thrust of his arousal just above the juncture of her legs. Any warning bells were lost in the rush of blood as her own hands went to Cruz's wide chest and then higher, until she was arching into him and winding her arms around his neck.

When his mouth left hers she gasped for air, light-headed, shivering as he transferred his attention to her neck, tugging at her skin gently with his teeth before soothing with his tongue.

Air touched her back as the zip of her dress was lowered. The bodice loosened around her breasts and she finally managed to open her eyes. Cruz's short hair was dishevelled, his eyes burning, as he pulled the top of her dress down, exposing her bare breasts to his gaze. The cut of the dress hadn't allowed for a bra.

'So beautiful,' he said thickly, bringing a hand up to cup the weight of one breast in his palm.

Trinity felt drunk…dazed. She looked down and saw her own pale flesh surrounded by his much darker hand. Her nipple jutted out, hard and stark, as if begging for his touch. When he brushed it with his thumb she let out a low moan and her head fell back.

Her arms were weakening around his neck and her legs were shaking. There was so much sensation on top of sensation. It was almost painful. And then suddenly the ground beneath her feet disappeared altogether and she gasped when she realised that Cruz had picked her up and was now laying her down on the nearby couch.

Her dress was gaping open and she felt disorientated yet hyper-alert. Cruz came down on his knees beside her supine body and pulled her dress all the way down to her waist, baring her completely.

She couldn't suck in enough air, and when he lowered that dark golden head and surrounded the taut peak of her breast with sucking heat her back arched and she gasped out loud, funnelling her hands through his hair…

She ignored the part of her whispering to stop this

now…she couldn't stop. She wasn't strong enough. She'd never felt so wanted and connected as she did right in that moment, and for Trinity that was where her darkest weakness lay. Still…

Cruz was drowning…in the sweetest, softest skin he'd ever felt or tasted in his life. The blood thundering through his veins and arteries made what he'd felt for any other woman a total mockery. It was as if he'd been existing in limbo and now he was alive again.

One hand was filled with the flesh of Trinity's breast, the hard nipple stabbing his palm, and he tugged the sharp point of her other breast into his mouth, his tongue laving the hard flesh, making it even harder. She tasted of sweet musky female and roses, and she felt like silk.

He wasn't even aware of her fingers clawing into his head so painfully. He was only aware of this pure decadent heaven, and the way she was arching her body at him so needily.

He finally let go of the fleshy mound of her breast and found her dress, pulling it up over her legs. He needed to feel her now, feel how ready for him she was. He wanted to taste her… His erection hardened even more at that thought.

He found her heat, palpable through the thin silk of her panties, and lifted his head, feeling animalistic at way she throbbed so hotly into his palm.

Trinity stopped moving. Her eyes opened and Cruz wanted to groan when he saw how sensually slumberous she looked, golden hair spread around her, breasts moving up and down, nipples moist from his touch. Mouth swollen from his kisses.

Giving in to his base needs, he moved down, pulling her dress up higher. Her panties were white and lacy and he pulled them off, heedless of the ripping sound, dropping them to the floor.

'Cruz...what are you doing...?'

She sounded breathless, rough. Needy. And there was some other quality to her voice that Cruz didn't want to investigate. Something like uncertainty.

'I need to taste you, *querida.*'

Her eyes widened. 'Taste me...? You mean like...?'

Cruz touched her with his finger, sliding it between soft silken folds. She gasped and tried to put her hand down, but he caught it and stopped her. He explored the hot damp seam of her body, pressing into the fevered channel of her body and exerting pressure against her clitoris.

He took his finger away, even though he wanted to thrust it all the way inside, and brought it to his mouth, taking the wet tip into his mouth. His eyes closed...his erection jumped. For the first time since he was a teenager Cruz was afraid he'd spill before he even got inside her.

The taste of her musky heat on his tongue...

He opened his eyes and she was looking at him, shocked. Two spots of red in her cheeks. A thought drifted across the heat haze in his brain... Why was she looking so shocked? Surely she'd...? But he batted the thought away, not wanting images of what she'd done with previous lovers—*his brother*—to intrude.

There would only be one lover now. Him. She was here and she was *his*.

He said in a rough voice, 'I need to taste you...like that.'

She said nothing. He saw her bite her lip. She looked feverish, and then she gave an almost imperceptible nod. Cruz pushed her legs apart, exposing the blonde curls covering her slick pink folds...slick for him.

There was none of his usual finesse when he touched her. He licked her, sucked and tasted, until he was dizzy and drunk. He thrust two fingers inside her heat, moving them in and out. He felt her hips jerk, her back arch. Heard soft moans and gasps, felt hands in his hair.

Her thighs drew up beside his head and her whole body tensed like a taut bow, just seconds before powerful muscles clamped down tight on his fingers and her body shuddered against his mouth.

She was *his*.

CHAPTER EIGHT

TRINITY WAS BARELY CONSCIOUS, floating on an ocean of such satisfaction that she wondered if she might be dead. Surely this wasn't even possible? This much pleasure? For her body to feel so weighted down and yet light as a feather? She could feel the minor contractions of her deepest muscles, still pulsing like little quivering heartbeats...

She finally came back to some level of consciousness when she felt a soft surface under her back and opened her eyes. She was on a bed, and Cruz was standing before her, pulling off his shirt and putting his hands on his trousers, undoing them, taking them down.

She saw the way his erection tented his underwear, and watched with avid fascination as he pulled that off too, exposing the thick stiff column of flesh, moisture beading at the tip.

'If you keep looking at me like that—' He broke off with a curse and bent down, hands on the sides of her dress, tugging it free of her body.

Trinity was naked now, and yet she felt no sense of self-consciousness. She was so wrapped in lingering pleasure and so caught up in this bubble of sensuality that she ignored the persistent but faint knocking of something trying to get through to her...

Cruz reached beside the bed for a condom and rolled it onto his erection, the latex stretched taut. Incredibly, as he came down onto the bed and moved over her, she felt her flesh quiver back to life. Her pulse picked up again and she no longer felt like floating...she wanted to fly again.

Cruz's hips pushed her legs apart and he took himself in his own hand, touching the head of his sex against hers, teasing her by pushing it in slightly before drawing it out again, her juices making them both slick. She felt as if she should be embarrassed, but she wasn't.

Between her legs she could feel her flesh aching for Cruz, aching for more than his mouth and tongue and fingers…aching for more.

She arched up. 'Please, Cruz…'

Was that ragged voice hers? She didn't have time to wonder, because with one feral growl and a sinuous move of his lean hips he thrust deep inside her. His whole body went taut over hers, and the expression on his face was one of pure masculine appreciation.

But Trinity wasn't seeing that. It had taken only a second for the intense need and pleasure to transform into blinding hot pain. She couldn't breathe, couldn't make sense of what she was feeling, when seconds ago she'd craved for him to do exactly this…

'*Dios,* Trinity…' he breathed. 'You're so tight…'

Cruz started to pull back, and Trinity's muscles protested. She put her hands on his hips and said, as panic mounted through her body along with the pain, 'Get off me! I can't…breathe…'

Cruz stopped moving instantly, shock in his voice. 'I'm hurting you?'

Her eyes were stinging now, as she sobbed while trying to push him off, '*Yes*, it hurts!'

He pulled away and Trinity let out a sound of pain. Cruz reared back, staring at her, and then down at something on the bed between them.

'What the hell—?'

She was starting to shiver in reaction and she looked down. The cover on the bed was cream, but even in the dim light she could see the spots of red—blood.

Her head started to whirl sickeningly as what had just happened sank in and she scrambled to move, almost falling off the bed in her bid to escape. She got to the bathroom and slammed the door behind her.

Cruz paced up and down after pulling on his trousers. There was nothing but ominous silence from the bathroom. His mind was fused with recrimination. He simply could not believe what her tight body and the evidence of blood told him. That she was innocent. That she was a virgin. It was like trying to compute the reality of seeing a unicorn, or a pig flying across the sky.

It simply wasn't possible. But then his conscience blasted him... He'd never been so lost in a haze of lust—he'd thought she was there with him, as ready as he was.

He wanted to go after her, but the sick realisation hit him that he was probably the last person she wanted to see right now. Nevertheless, he went and knocked softly on the door. 'Trinity?'

Silence.

Just when Cruz was about to try and open the door she said, 'I'm fine. I just need a minute.'

Cruz's hand clenched into a fist at the way her voice sounded so rough. He took a step back from the door and then he heard the sound of the shower being turned on. His guts curdled. Was she trying to wash him off her?

He'd never been in this situation before. He'd never slept with a virgin before...

And then his mind went on that disbelieving loop again—how was it even possible? She'd been his brother's *wife*!

Cruz sat down on the end of the bed and a grim expression settled over his features as he waited for Trinity to come out of the bathroom and explain what the hell was going on.

Trinity sat on the floor of the shower stall, knees pulled into her chest, arms wrapped around them and her head resting on the wall behind her, eyes closed as the hot water sluiced down over her skin. She couldn't stop shivering, and all she could see was the shock on Cruz's face.

Between her legs it still stung slightly, but the red-hot pain had gone. And yet along with that pain Trinity had felt something else—something on the edges of the pain, promising more—but the shock of realising that Cruz was witnessing her ultimate exposure had eclipsed any desire to keep going.

She opened her eyes and saw nothing but steam. In the heated rush of more pleasure and sensations than she'd ever known, maybe she'd hoped that Cruz wouldn't realise...

But he had. And what she'd experienced before when he'd rejected her was nothing compared to the prospect of how he would look at her now.

When Trinity emerged a short time later, wrapped in a thick towelling robe, Cruz stood up from where he'd been sitting on the end of the bed. He looked as pale as she felt, and something quivered inside her.

His chest was bare, and it was if she hadn't really seen it the first time he'd bared it. She'd been so consumed with desire. It was wide, with defined musculature and dark golden hair covering his pectorals, leading down in a line between an impressive six-pack to arrow under his trousers. A glorious example of a masculine male in his prime.

'Trinity...?'

She looked at his face and saw an expression she'd never seen before—something between contrition and bewilderment.

'I'm sorry,' she said, her voice husky.

Now something more familiar crossed his face—irritation. 'Why the hell didn't you tell me that you were still a virgin?'

She wanted to curl up in a corner, but she stood tall. 'I didn't think you'd notice.'

He frowned. 'How could I not have noticed?'

He seemed to go even paler for a second, as if he was remembering what it had been like to breach that secret and intimate defence. And that only made Trinity remember it too—the pain and then that other tantalising promise of pleasure…hovering on the edges. How amazing it had felt up to that point. How lost she'd been, dizzy with need and lust. Forgetting everything. Forgetting that she needed to protect herself from this…

She went to move past him. 'I don't really want to talk about this now.'

He caught her arm as she was passing. 'Wait just a second—'

'Look, I *really* don't want to talk about this right now.' She felt flayed all over, and way too vulnerable.

Cruz's hand tightened on her arm. 'I deserve an explanation. *Dios*, Trinity, I *hurt* you. And you were married to my brother—how the hell are you still a virgin?'

Her heart slammed against her ribs. This was it. The moment when Cruz would *have* to listen to her. Because of the irrefutable physical humiliation she'd just handed him on a plate.

She turned to face him and looked up. Her voice was husky with emotion. 'I've been trying to explain to you all along that it wasn't a real marriage, Cruz, but you didn't want to hear it. It was a marriage of convenience.'

There was silence for a long moment. The lines of Cruz's face were incredibly stark and grim. He said, 'I'm listening now.'

Trinity's legs felt wobbly and she sat down on the edge of the bed, seeing the stain of her innocence on the sheets in her peripheral vision.

Her cheeks burning, she gestured with her hand. 'I should do something with the sheet—the stain—'

'Can wait,' Cruz said with steel in his tone. 'Talk, Trinity, you owe me an explanation.'

Anger surged up, because if he'd been prepared to listen to her weeks ago they could have avoided this scene, but it dissipated under his stern look. In truth, how hard had she really tried to talk to him? Had she been happy just to let him think the worst so she could avoid him seeing how pathetic she really was? Contriving to make a home out of a fake marriage with children who weren't even her own?

'Okay,' Cruz said, when the words still wouldn't come. 'Why don't we start with this: why did you go to work for Rio? I hadn't fired you.'

She looked up at him. 'How could I have stayed working for you after what had happened? I was embarrassed.' Realising that she'd reached peak humiliation, she said bitterly, 'I had a crush on you, Cruz. I was the worst kind of cliché. A lowly maid lusting after her gorgeous and unattainable boss. When you rejected me that night—'

'I told you,' he interrupted. 'I did not reject you. I hated myself for crossing a line and taking advantage of you.'

Trinity stood up, incensed. 'You asked me if I regularly walked around the house in my nightclothes, as if I'd done it on purpose!'

A dull flush scored along Cruz's cheekbones. 'I didn't handle the situation well. I was angry... But it was with myself. Not you—no matter how it sounded.'

Refusing to be mollified, Trinity said, 'The following night you gave me that look as you greeted the beautiful brunette... You were sending me a message not to get any ideas. Not to forget that what had happened was a huge mistake.'

Cruz ran his hands through his hair impatiently, all his

muscles taut. 'I don't even remember who that was. All I could see was you and that hurt look on your face.'

Trinity's cheeks burned even hotter. She'd been so obvious.

She continued, 'At one point during the evening I went outside. Rio was there, smoking a cigarette. He saw that I was upset and he asked me why...so I told him. He seemed nice. Kind. And then...then he told me that he was looking for a new nanny. He asked me if I'd be interested... and I said yes. I couldn't imagine staying in your house knowing that every time you looked at me it would be with pity and regret.'

Cruz's eyes burned. 'And yet after six months you were his wife?'

Trinity sat down again on the bed. 'Yes.'

Cruz was pacing back and forth now, sleek muscles moving sinuously under olive skin. Distracting.

He stopped. 'So do you want to tell me how you went from nanny to convenient wife?'

She'd wanted this moment to come, hadn't she? And yet she felt reluctant. Because she knew she'd be revealing something of Rio to Cruz that would tarnish him in his eyes, and even after everything she was loath to do that.

But she didn't have a choice now.

She took a breath. 'I'd gone out to the cinema one night. Rio had assured me he had no plans and that he'd be home all evening. When I got back the twins were awake in their room and hysterical. Their nappies were soaking and I don't think they'd been fed. It took me a couple of hours to calm them down, feed them and put them down again. Frankly, it terrified me that they'd been in that state. I went downstairs and found Rio passed out over his desk, drunk. I managed to wake him up and get some coffee into him... but it was clear then that he was in no fit shape to be left alone with his sons—ever.'

Cruz looked shocked. 'I know Rio liked to indulge, but I never would have thought he'd do it while looking after his sons.'

Trinity sucked in a breath. 'I threatened to tell the police…even call you…but Rio begged me not to. He said it was a one-off. I told him I couldn't stand by and let him neglect his children and he begged me to listen to him before I did anything. He told me what had happened to him as a child. He told me he wasn't a perfect father but that he didn't want his boys to be taken into care.'

Trinity looked at Cruz.

'He knew about my past…where I'd come from. I'd told him not long after I started working for him.' Her mouth compressed at the memory of her naivety. 'He seemed to have an ability to unearth people's secrets. And he used that to make me feel guilty for even suggesting that I'd report him. That I would risk subjecting his sons to the same experience I'd had.'

Cruz interjected. 'I would never have let that happen.'

'You were on the other side of the world,' Trinity pointed out. 'And Rio didn't want me to tell you what had happened. I knew you weren't close, so how could I go behind his back?'

She stood up, feeling agitated. Pacing back and forth, aware of Cruz's preternatural stillness.

'But then suddenly he was offering me a solution—to marry him. It was crazy, ridiculous, but somehow he made it seem…logical.'

She stopped and faced Cruz.

'He promised that it would be strictly in name only. He told me he'd hire a nanny to help. He said he wanted to appear more settled, to prove to people that he wasn't just a useless playboy. He said that in return for taking care of the boys and going to some social functions with him I could name my price. Whatever I wanted…'

Something gleamed in Cruz's eyes. 'What was it, Trinity? What did you want?'

She hated it that even now Cruz seemed to be waiting for her to expose herself. She lifted her chin. 'I told him I'd always wanted to go to college. To get a degree. And so he promised to fund my course once the boys were a little older and in a more settled routine.'

Cruz looked at her for a long moment and then shook his head. 'I don't get it. Even with the promise of fulfilling your college dream, why would you agree to a marriage like that unless you were going to get a lot more out of it? Evidently you didn't sleep with Rio, but did you want to? Did you plan on seducing him? Making the marriage real?'

Disappointment vied with anger. 'You will never believe me, will you? Even when you have to admit that I'm not a gold-digger, your cynicism just won't let you...'

She went to walk out of the room, but Cruz caught her arm. She stopped and gritted her jaw against the reaction in her body.

Cruz pulled her around to face him, but before he could say anything, she inserted defensively, 'Of course I wasn't planning on seducing Rio. I had no interest in him like that, and he had no interest in me.'

She looked down for a moment, her damp hair slipping over one shoulder, but Cruz caught her chin between his thumb and forefinger, tipping it back up. Not letting her escape. There was something different in his eyes now—something that made her heart flip-flop.

He just said, '*Why*, Trinity?'

She felt as if he could see right down into the deepest part of her, where she had nothing left to hide.

She pulled her chin away from his hand and said, 'I felt a sense of affinity with him...with the fact that in spite of our differences we had a lot in common.' Her voice turned husky. 'But the largest part of why I agreed was because I'd

come to love Matty and Sancho. They needed me.' Afraid
that the next thing she'd see on Cruz's face would be pity,
Trinity said, 'I'm well aware that my motivations had a
lot to do with my own experiences, but I'm not afraid to
admit that. They had no one else to look out for them, and
I believed I was doing the right thing by them.'

She tried to pull her arm free of Cruz's grip but it only
tightened.

She glared at him, hating him for making her reveal so
much. 'Just let me go, Cruz. Now you know everything…
and I know that after what just happened you won't want
a repeat performance…so can we just put it behind us?
Please?'

He frowned. 'Won't want a repeat performance?'

He pulled her closer. Her breath hitched and her heart
started pounding.

'I hurt you, Trinity. If I'd known it was your first time
I would have been much more gentle.'

She looked away, humiliation curdling her insides. 'You
really don't have to pity me, Cruz. You came to your senses
after kissing me that first time. I was unsuitable before and
now I'm *really* unsuitable.'

Trinity had managed to pull her arm free and take a couple
of steps towards the door when Cruz acted on blind instinct
and grabbed her waist and hauled her back, trapping her
against him with his arms around her body.

He was reeling from everything that had just trans-
pired—the sheer fact of Trinity's physical innocence was
like a bomb whose aftershocks were still being felt. He
didn't like to admit it, but the knowledge that her marriage to Rio hadn't been real… It eclipsed everything else
at that moment, making a ragged and torn part of him feel
whole again.

Trinity put her hands on his arms and tried to push,

but he wouldn't let her go. *Not now. Not ever*, whispered a voice. Base desires were overwhelming his need to analyse everything she'd just said. *Later.* When his brain had cleared.

She said in a frigid voice, 'Let me go, Cruz.'

He turned her so she was facing him. Her face was flushed, eyes huge. He felt feral as he said, 'Believe me when I say that the last thing I feel for you is pity, Trinity. Or that you're unsuitable. And you're wrong, you know…'

'Wrong about what?' She sounded shaky.

Looking down at her now, some of the cravening need Cruz was feeling dissipated as his chest tightened with an emotion he'd never expected, nor welcomed. But this woman evoked it effortlessly, especially after the shattering revelations of her innocence, and in more ways than one.

He shook his head, honesty compelling him to say, 'I haven't come to my senses since that night. You've bewitched me, Trinity.'

'What do you mean?'

Cruz knew that he'd never before willingly stepped into a moment of emotional intimacy like this. No other woman had ever come close enough to precipitate it. After everything that had just happened he felt exposed and raw, in a way that should have been making him feel seriously claustrophobic, but what he *was* feeling was…a kind of liberation.

'What I mean is that I haven't looked at another woman since that night.' His voice turned rough as he admitted, 'I haven't *wanted* another woman since I touched you.'

Her eyes widened. Her mouth closed and then opened again. Finally she said, 'You're not just saying this?'

Her vulnerability was laid bare, and Cruz wondered bleakly how he'd blocked it out before now.

Because he'd wanted to. Because it had been easier to believe the worst rather than let himself think for a second that she could possibly be as pure as he'd believed from the start. Because then he'd have had to acknowledge how she made him feel.

He shook his head. 'No, I'm not just saying this. You're all I want, Trinity. I hated thinking of you and Rio together... I was jealous of my own brother.'

Trinity felt breathless at Cruz's admission. She could see how hard it was for him to open up like this, even as it soothed a raw hurt inside her. And with that came the heavy knowledge that he was beating himself up now over feeling jealous of Rio—and that was exactly the result Rio had wanted to achieve. To mess with Cruz's head.

Loath to shatter this fragile moment, Trinity pushed that knowledge down deep, like a coward, and said, 'We were never together...not like that.' Feeling absurdly shy, she said, 'No other man has ever made me feel like you did. After...that night... I couldn't stop thinking about you... about how it would have been...'

'If we hadn't stopped?'

She nodded jerkily.

He gathered her closer and a tremor ran through her body. The air shifted around them, tension tightening again. 'We don't have to stop now...'

Trinity couldn't battle the desire rising inside her—not after what he'd just told her. She was already laid bare. Nowhere to hide any more. And she wanted this—wanted to fulfil this fantasy more than she wanted to take her next breath.

She looked up at him and fell into molten amber heat. 'Then don't stop, Cruz. Please.'

He waited for an infinitesimal moment and then lowered his head, touching his firm mouth to her softer one with a kind of reverence that made emotion bloom in her chest. To counteract it, because she wasn't remotely ready to deal with what it meant, she reached up and twined her arms around his neck, pressing closer, telling him with her body what she wanted...

He deepened the kiss, stroking into her mouth with an explicitness that made her groan softly, excitement mounting again. His hands moved around to her front, unknotting her robe. He pushed it apart and spread his hands on her hips, tracing her curves, before she broke away from the kiss, breathing raggedly.

He pulled back and looked at her, before pushing her robe off completely. Without looking away, he opened his trousers and pushed them down, kicking them off. Now they were both naked. Trinity looked down and her eyes widened. That stiff column of flesh jerked under her look, and a sense of very feminine wonder and sensuality filled her at the thought that she could have an effect on him like this.

He took her hand and brought it to his hard flesh, wrapping her fingers around him. Slowly, gently, he guided her, moving her hand up and down... It was heady, the way her skin glided over steely strength...

Cruz felt beads of perspiration pop out on his forehead as Trinity's untutored touch drove him to the edge of any reason he had left. It was a special kind of torture...and before she could reduce him to rubble he took her hand from him and led her to the bed.

He wanted to consume her until she was boneless and pliant and *his*.

When he laid her down on the bed and came down alongside her she reached out a tentative hand and touched his chest.

He sucked in a breath. 'Yes...touch me.'

His eyes devoured her perfect curves, slender and yet lush all at once. An intoxicating mix. Innocent and siren.

Innocent.

She laid her hand flat on his pectoral, and then bent her head and put her tongue to the blunt nub of his nipple. Cruz tensed. He'd never even known he was sensitive there. Small teeth nibbled gently at his flesh and his erection grew even harder at the certainty that she would be a quick study...that she would send him to orbit and back all too easily.

A fleeting moment of vulnerability was gone as she explored further and took him in her hand again, moving over his flesh with more confidence.

He groaned and put his hand over hers. She looked at him—suddenly unsure—and it made his chest squeeze. 'If you keep touching me like that I won't last...and I need to.'

'Oh,' she said, a blush staining her cheeks.

Cruz cupped her chin and said roughly, 'Come here.'

She moved up and his arm came around her. He hauled her into him so that she half lay on him, breasts pressed against his side. Her nipples scraped against his chest. Cruz pressed a hot kiss to her mouth, his tongue tangling lazily with hers, revelling in the lush feel of her body against his and the taste of her.

When he could feel her moving against him subtly, he gently pushed her back so that he was looking down at her. Her sheer beauty reached out and grabbed him deep inside, transcending the physical for a moment. Her eyes were wide and her pupils dilated. Her cheeks were flushed and her hair was spread around her head like a golden halo.

She was perfection. And everything she'd told him, if it was true— Cruz shut his mind down. He couldn't go there now.

He explored her body with a thoroughness that made her writhe against him, begging and pleading. But there was no way he wasn't going to make sure she was so ready for him that when they came together there would be no pain. Only pleasure.

He smoothed his hand over her belly, down to where her legs were shut tight. He bent his head again, kissing her deeply, and as he did so he gently pushed them apart and felt her moist heat against his palm.

He cupped her sex, letting her get used to him touching her there, and explored along the seam of her body, releasing her heat, opening her to him with his fingers. He moved his fingers in and out. He could feel her body grow taut, and then he lifted his head to look down at her.

'Come for me, Trinity...'

And as if primed to do his bidding, she did, tipping over the edge with a low, keening cry. He had to exert extreme control to stop himself from spilling at the stunning beauty of her response.

Her hand was gripping his arm, and he could feel her body pulsating around his fingers. He looked at her for a long moment and said, 'If you don't want to go any further now, that's okay.'

Her eyes opened and it seemed to take her a second to focus on him. She shook her head. 'No, I'm okay. Keep going...'

Cruz sent up a prayer of thanks to some god he'd never consulted before. He reached over her to get protection from the drawer. When he was sheathed, he came up on his knees between her legs, pushing them apart, hands huge on her thighs.

Cruz came forward, bracing himself on one hand on the bed beside her, and with his other hand notched the head of his erection against her body, using her arousal to ease his passage into her. He teased her like this until she started panting a little, and arching herself towards him.

Unable to wait a second longer, slowly, inch by inch, he sank into her body, watching her face. She stared up at him, focused, and something inside him turned over even as all he could think about was how perfect it felt to have his body filling hers.

And then, when Cruz was so deep inside her that he could barely breathe, he started to move in and out, with achingly slow precision. She wrapped one of her legs around his waist and he had to clench his jaw as it deepened his penetration.

'I'm okay…' she breathed. 'It feels…good.'

He couldn't hold back. The movements of his body became faster, more urgent. Trinity was biting her lip, her pale skin dewed with perspiration. Cruz reached under her and hitched her hips up towards him, deepening his thrusts even more. Trinity groaned.

'That's it, *querida*, come with me.'

When she shattered this time it was so powerful that he shattered with her, deep inside her, his whole body curving over hers as they rode out the storm together.

Trinity woke slowly from a delicious dream, in which she had arms wrapped tight around her and she was imbued with an incredible sense of acceptance, belonging, safety, home.

Trust.

As soon as that little word reverberated in her head, though, she woke up. She was in Cruz's bedroom, amongst tangled sheets, and her whole body was one big pleasurable ache.

And she was alone.

When that registered it *all* came back.

Trinity's sense of euphoria and well-being faded as she recalled telling Cruz *everything*.

She'd trusted him with her deepest vulnerabilities.

Trust. Trinity went even colder as the magnitude of that

sank in. She'd let Cruz into a space inside her that had been locked up for as long as she could remember.

Trust was not her friend. Trust had got her where she was today. First of all she'd trusted herself to follow her instincts and allow Cruz to kiss her that night. Then she'd trusted Rio, believing his motives for hiring her and marrying her were transparent and benign. Instead he'd manipulated her into becoming a tool of destruction against Cruz.

And now that urge was whispering to her again...to trust Cruz just because he'd made her body weep with more pleasure than she'd ever known could be possible. And because he'd admitted that he hadn't been with another woman since that night in his study. Since he'd kissed her.

Just remembering that now made her chest grow tight all over again. She'd never expected him to say that. What if it had just been a line, though? To get her back into bed? And she, like the fool, had believed him...

Feeling panicky now, at the thought of Cruz suddenly appearing and finding her when she felt so raw, she got out of bed and slipped on a robe. She picked up her severely crumpled dress, her face burning.

There was no sign of him as she went back to her room, and after a quick shower and changing into clean clothes she went into the main part of the apartment. She was very conscious of her body—still tender in private places—and it only made her feel more vulnerable. As if Cruz had branded her.

She knew he wasn't there even before she saw that it was empty and an acute sense of disappointment vied with relief. What had she wanted? To wake up with his arms around her? *Yes*, whispered a voice, and Trinity castigated herself. Men like Cruz didn't indulge in such displays of affection.

Her phone pinged from her bag nearby just then, and Trinity took it out to see a text from Cruz. Instantly her heart skipped a beat. Scowling at herself she read it.

I had an early-morning meeting and some things have come up so I'm going to stay in Madrid for another day/ night. My driver is downstairs and he will take you to the airport where the plane is waiting whenever you are ready. Cruz.

Trinity dithered for a few minutes before writing back.

Okay.

She almost put an automatic *x* in the text, but stopped herself just in time.

A couple of minutes later there was another ping from her phone. She put down the coffee she'd just poured to read the text.

Just okay?

Feeling irritated at the mocking tone she could almost hear, she wrote back.

Okay. Fine.

Ping.

How are you feeling this morning?

Trinity's face was burning now. She would bet that Cruz didn't text his other lovers like this. They'd know how to play the game and be cool.

She wrote back.

Totally fine. Same as yesterday.

Ping.

Liar.

She responded.

I thought you had meetings to go to?

Ping.

I'm in one. It's boring.

Trinity was smiling before she stopped herself and wrote back.

Okay, if you must know I'm a little tender, but it feels nice.

She sent it before she had time to change her mind, feeling giddy.
Ping.

Good.

Not knowing how to respond to that smug response, Trinity put the phone down and took a deep breath. Her phone pinged again and she jumped.

Cursing Cruz, she picked it up.

We'll talk when I get back to the castillo.

The giddiness Trinity had been feeling dissipated like a burst balloon. She went cold. Of course they would talk. He'd had a chance to process what she'd told him now, and she could imagine that he didn't appreciate her telling him those less than savoury things about Rio.

That wasn't even the half of it. He didn't know the full extent of just how much Rio had despised him.

Trinity wrote back.

Okay.

Cruz didn't respond. She left the coffee untouched and put her arms around herself as the full enormity of what had happened the previous night sank in. She walked to the huge window in the living room and stared out, unseeing.

The prospect of Cruz going over what she'd told him and digging any deeper than he'd already done, finding out the true depth of hatred that Rio had harboured for him, made her go icy all over. She couldn't do that to him.

And that was the scariest revelation of all. The intensity of the emotion swelling in her chest told her she was in deep trouble. The walls she'd erected around herself from a young age to protect herself in uncaring environments were no longer standing—they were dust.

First two small brown-eyed imps had burrowed their way in, stealing her heart, and now—

She put a hand to her chest and sucked in a pained breath. She could no longer claim to hate Cruz for what he'd done in forcing her into this marriage—if she ever truly had.

From the start she'd been infatuated with him, even after what she'd perceived to be his rejection of her. And then she'd seen a side to him that had mocked her for feeling tender towards him. But hadn't he shown her last night that he could be tender? Achingly so.

And, as much as she was scared that he'd just spun her a line about there being no women since he'd kissed her, just to get her into bed, she realised that she *did* trust him. He was too full of integrity to lie about something like that. He didn't need to.

And that left her teetering on the edge of a very scary precipice—although if she was brutally honest with herself she'd fallen over the edge a long time ago. Right about the time when Cruz had insisted on her going to bed so that he could sit up with the twins and she'd found herself yearning to be part of that tableau. *A family*...

She whirled away from the window, suddenly needing to leave and get back to the *castillo*—put some physical space between her and Cruz. One thing was uppermost in her mind—there couldn't be a repeat of last night. She wasn't strong enough to withstand Cruz's singular devastating focus and then survive when he got bored or decided to move on—which he would undoubtedly do.

For the first time, shamefully, Trinity had to admit to feeling unsure of her ability to sacrifice her own desires for the sake of Matty and Sancho. And she hated Cruz for doing this to her. Except...she didn't.

She loved them all and it might just kill her.

CHAPTER NINE

TRINITY HATED FEELING so nervous. She smoothed her hand down over the linen material of her buttoned shirt-dress. She'd changed after Julia had come to tell her that Cruz was back and wanted to see her.

She hated that she wondered if it was a bad omen that Cruz hadn't come looking for her himself. If not for her, then for the boys, who'd been asking for him constantly.

Cursing her vacillation, she lifted her hand and knocked on his study door, feeling a sense of déjà-vu when she heard him say, 'Come in.'

She went in and saw Cruz was behind the desk. He stood up, his gaze raking her up and down, making her skin tingle. She was conscious of her bare legs. Plain sandals. Hair tied back.

She closed the door behind her.

Cruz gestured to a chair. 'Come in…sit down.'

His voice sounded rough and it impacted on her.

She walked over and took the seat, feeling awkward. Not knowing where to look but unable to look away from those spectacular eyes and that tall, broad body. Remembering how it had felt when he'd surged between her legs, filling her—

Cruz sat down too. 'How are the boys?'

Trinity fought against the blush she could feel spreading across her chest and up into her face. Sometimes she really hated her colouring.

'They're fine… They were asking for you, wondering where you were.'

An expression that was curiously vulnerable flashed

across Cruz's face. 'I'll go and see them later,' he said. 'How are you?' he asked then.

Trinity fought not to squirm. 'I'm fine.'

An altogether more carnal look came across his face now. 'No...soreness?'

Trinity couldn't stop the blush this time. 'No.'

The carnal look faded and suddenly Cruz stood up again, running a hand through his hair. Trinity's gaze drank him in, registering that he must have changed when he got back as he was wearing soft jeans and a polo shirt.

When he didn't say anything for a moment she dragged her gaze up to his face and went still. He looked tortured.

She stood up, immediately concerned. 'What is it?'

He looked at her. 'I owe you an apology...on behalf of me *and* my brother.'

She went very still, almost afraid to say the words. 'You believe me, then...?'

Cruz paced for a moment, and then stopped and faced her again. He looked angry, but she could recognise that it wasn't with her.

'Of course I do.'

She sat down again on the chair behind her, her legs suddenly feeling weak. She waited for a feeling of vindication but it didn't come. She just felt a little numb.

Cruz shook his head. 'After Rio died I took everything his solicitor told me for granted. The truth was that I was in shock...grieving. Based on what he'd told me, I believed you deserved to be the focus of my anger and resentment, so I didn't do what I should have done—which was to investigate his finances with a fine-tooth comb. I've started to do that now,' he said heavily, 'and I had my own legal team haul in his solicitor for questioning yesterday. That's why I stayed behind in Madrid.'

Trinity's throat moved as she swallowed. 'What did you find?'

'Did you know he was a chronic gambler?'

She shook her head, shocked. 'No, of course not… He was away a lot. And worked odd hours. He never really explained himself.'

Cruz was grim. 'He hid it very well. It seems that as soon as he knew what was happening he spent even more money, and he started putting your name on things—like authorising the redecoration of the house, ordering credit cards in your name but using them himself…'

Trinity breathed in, feeling sick. 'So *that* was the trail directly back to me?'

Cruz nodded. 'He made sure you were seen out and about, at fashion shows and events, so if anyone ever questioned him he could point to you and say that you'd been instrumental in his downfall.' Cruz continued, 'You shouldn't feel like he duped you too easily—he did it to countless others along the way. Including me. If I hadn't been so blinkered where Rio was concerned, and had looked into his affairs before now—'

'Then you wouldn't have felt obliged to marry me because you'd have known I wasn't a threat,' Trinity said quickly.

She was avoiding his eye now and Cruz came over.

'Look at me,' he commanded.

After an infinitesimal moment she did, hoping her emotions weren't showing.

'I'm Matty and Sancho's uncle, and I'm going to be in their lives. You are the only mother my nephews have known and I was always going to come back here. Marriage was the best option.'

Trinity felt herself flinch minutely. *Marriage was the best option.* Suddenly feeling exposed under that amber gaze, she stood up and stepped around the chair in a bid to put some space between them. He was too close.

'We haven't finished this conversation,' he said warningly.

Her need to self-protect was huge. 'I think we have. You've said sorry and I accept your apology.'

'There's more, though, isn't there?' he asked now, folding his arms. 'That night—the night of the party at my house—you wanted to tell me something but I shut you down. What was it, exactly?'

Trinity felt panicky and took a step back towards the door. 'It was just my concerns about Rio—he'd been acting irrationally and I was worried, and we'd had that row—' She stopped suddenly and Cruz seized on it.

'You had a row? What about?'

She cursed her mouth and recognised the intractability in Cruz. He wouldn't let this go. He'd physically stopped her leaving before, and if he touched her now...

Reluctantly she said, 'I'd confronted him about being so...erratic. He was spending no time with the boys. He was drinking. And I'm sure he was doing drugs. I threatened to call you and tell you I was worried.'

Rio had sneered at her. *Go on, run to lover boy and cry on his shoulder and you'll see how interested he still is. Cruz doesn't care about you, or me. He only cares about the precious De Carrillo legacy. The legacy that's mine!*

'What did he say?'

Trinity forced herself out of the past. 'He said that if I did anything of the sort he'd divorce me and never let me see Matty or Sancho again, and that he'd ruin any chances for my future employment, not to mention my chances of going to college.'

Cruz said, 'That must have been just after I'd returned to London. I'd asked to meet him—I'd been alerted by our accountants that he was haemorrhaging money. That's when he told me those lies about you and blamed you for pretty much everything. I had no reason not to believe him when there were all those receipts and the evidence of your social lifestyle…'

Trinity felt unaccountably bitter to hear Cruz confirming all this. She was also shocked at one person's ability to be so cruel. Without thinking, she said, 'He used me because he wanted to get back at you. He wanted to make you jealous because he—' She stopped suddenly, eyes fixed guiltily on Cruz.

What was wrong with her? It was as if she physically couldn't keep the truth back.

'Because he *what*?' Cruz asked, eyes narrowed on her flaming face.

She backed away, feeling sick. 'Nothing.'

Cruz was grim as he effortlessly reached for her, caught her by the hands and pulled her back, forcing her back down into the chair and keeping her hands in one of his.

'Tell me, Trinity. I know there's more to it than just the fact that Rio was going off the rails. He'd been going off the rails ever since he got his inheritance and, believe me, I know that's my fault.'

She looked up at him, momentarily distracted. Anger rushed through her because Cruz felt such irrational guilt over someone who didn't deserve it. Especially when that guilt had blinkered him to Rio's true nature and crimes.

She pulled her hands back, resting them on her lap. 'That wasn't your fault, Cruz. I lived with him for a year and a half, so I should know. Rio was selfish and self-absorbed, and all that inheritance did was highlight his flaws.'

Cruz looked at her carefully. 'There's still more.'

She shook her head, desperately wishing he'd drop it. 'No, there's not.'

He grabbed a nearby chair and pulled it over to sit down right in front of her, all but trapping her. Their knees were touching and she was very conscious of her bare legs under the dress. It didn't help when his gaze dropped momentarily to her chest.

He looked up again and arched a brow. She scowled at him. 'You can't force me to talk.'

'You'll talk, Trinity, and if you don't want to talk then we'll find other ways to occupy our time until you do.'

He put a hand on her bare knee, sliding it up her thigh until she slapped her hand down on his. He gripped her thigh and she felt a betraying pulse throb between her legs.

'Your choice. Either way, you're talking.'

She was between a rock and a hard place. If Cruz touched her she'd go up in flames and might not be able to hold back her emotions. But if she told him the truth about Rio, and he realised why she'd been so reluctant to tell him...

But he deserved to know—however hard it was. However much she wished she didn't have to.

She blurted out, 'I don't want to tell you because I don't want to hurt you.'

Cruz looked at her. Trinity couldn't have said anything more shocking. No one had ever said such a thing to him because no one had ever cared about hurting him before. Certainly not a lover, because he was always very careful not to give them that power.

But right now he could feel his insides contracting, as if to ward off a blow. Instinctively he wanted to move back, but he didn't. 'What are you talking about?'

Her eyes were like two blue bruises.

'Rio set me up way before he needed to use me to blame for his money problems.' She felt her face grow hot as she admitted, 'He offered me the job because he saw an opportunity to distract you, to make you jealous. He told me when we had the row that he'd hated you for as long as he could remember, but that he'd managed to make you believe he was grateful for the hand-outs he said you gave him.'

Cruz forced himself to say, 'Go on.'

'His ultimate ambition was to take you over—to use the marriage and his sons as evidence that he was the more stable heir. That he could be trusted. He wanted to see you humiliated, punished for being the legitimate heir. He never got over his resentment of you, Cruz.'

He realised dimly that he should be feeling hurt, exactly as Trinity had said. But it wasn't hurt he was feeling. It was a sense of loss—the loss of something he'd never had. And that realisation was stark and painful.

Trinity was looking at him and he couldn't breathe. He took his hand off her thigh and moved back, standing up. A sense of inarticulate anger rushed up...that awful futility.

Trinity stood too, and she was pale, and it made his anger snap even more. An irrational urge to lash out gripped him. A need to push her back to a safe distance, where it wouldn't feel as if her eyes could see right down to the depths of his very soul.

'You have to admit,' he said now, 'things worked out for you remarkably well, considering. You still managed to elevate yourself from humble maid to nanny to wife. You may have proved your physical innocence, but can I really trust that you weren't the one who saw your opportunity that night when you spoke to Rio? Maybe you followed him into the garden?'

'No!'

She shook her head, and now there was fire in her eyes as well as something far more disturbing. Something that twisted Cruz's guts.

'*No*. I was hurt, and I was naive enough to let him see it...and he took advantage of that.'

All Cruz could see was her. Beautiful. Injured. *His*

fault. The desire to push her back faded as quickly as it had come on.

Acting on instinct, he went over to her, chest tight. The desk was behind her—she couldn't move. Cruz took her face in his hands, lifting it up. 'Who are you, Trinity Adams? Is it really possible that you're that wide-eyed naive girl who turned up in my office looking for a chance? Full of zeal and a kind of innocence I've never seen before?'

Cruz's character assessment of her chafed unbearably, and Trinity balled her hands into fists at her sides.

'Yes,' she said, in a low voice throbbing with pain. 'I was that stupidly naive girl who was so starved for a sense of belonging that at the first sign of it she toppled right over the edge.'

She hated it that his proximity was making her melt even as hurt and anger twisted and roiled in her gut.

She took his hands down off her face. 'Just let me go, Cruz... There's nothing more to discuss. There's nothing between us.'

She felt his body go rigid and saw his eyes burn.

'You're wrong. There isn't nothing—there's this.'

His mouth was over hers before she could take another breath and Trinity went up in flames. Panic surged. She couldn't let this happen.

She tore her mouth away. 'Stop, Cruz, this isn't enough.'

'It's more than enough, *querida,* and it's enough for now.'

He started undoing the buttons of her shirt-dress, exposing her breasts in her lacy bra, dragging one cup down and thumbing her nipple. She wanted to tell him to *stop* again, but it was too late. She was tipping over the edge of not caring and into wanting this more. Anything to assuage the ache in her heart.

He lifted her with awesome ease onto the side of his

desk. She heard something fall to the floor and smash, but it was lost in the inferno consuming them. He was yanking open her dress completely now...buttons were popping and landing on the floor.

He captured her mouth again as he pushed the dress off her shoulders and down her arms, pulling her bra down completely so her breasts were upthrust by the wire and exposed. The belt was still around her waist—the only thing keeping her dress attached to her body.

He palmed her breast as he stroked his tongue along hers, thrusting, mimicking a more intimate form of penetration. Trinity groaned into his mouth, instinctively arching her back to push her breast into his palm more fully, gasping when he trapped a hard nipple between his fingers before squeezing tightly.

She blindly felt for his T-shirt, pushing it up until they had to break apart so he could lift it off. He dropped it to the floor and Trinity reached for his jeans, snapping open the top button, aware of the bulge pressing against the zip. Heat flooded her—and urgency.

She was hampered when Cruz bent down and tongued a nipple, his hand going between her legs, spreading her thighs and pushing aside her panties to explore along her cleft. He pulled her forward slightly, so that she was on the edge of the desk, feet just touching the ground.

He slowly thrust one finger in and out, while torturing her breasts with his mouth and tongue. She was throbbing all over, slick and ready. The previous emotional whirlwind was blissfully forgotten in this moment of heated insanity.

'Please, Cruz...'

He looked up, his face stark with need. He undid his jeans and pushed them down and his erection sprang fee. Trinity took it in her hand, the moisture at the tip wetting her palm.

Cruz settled himself between her legs, the head of his

erection sliding against her sex, and it was too much. She was ready to beg when he tipped her back and notched himself into her heat. They both groaned, and he rested his forehead on hers for a moment.

Then he said, 'Wrap your legs around my waist.'

She did, barely aware that her sandals had fallen off. Cruz pulled her panties to one side and with one earth-shattering movement thrust into her, deep enough to steal her breath and her soul for ever.

He put an arm around her and hauled her even closer as he slowly thrust in and out, each glide of his body inside hers driving them higher and higher to the peak. She wrapped one arm around his neck, the other around his waist, struggling to stay rooted.

'Look at me,' he commanded roughly.

She opened her eyes and tipped back her head. The look on his face made a spasm of pure lust rush through her. It was feral. Desperate. Hungry. *Raw.*

Their movements became rougher...something else fell to the floor.

Cruz pushed her back onto the table, lying her flat, and took her hands in one of his, holding them above her head as he kept up the relentless rhythm of their bodies. She dug her heels into his buttocks, biting her lip to stop from screaming as the coil of tension wound so tight she thought she couldn't bear it any longer. But just at that moment he drew her nipple into his mouth, sucking fiercely, and the tension shattered to pieces and Trinity soared free of the bond that had been holding her so tight.

Cruz's body tensed over hers and she felt the hot burst of his release inside her.

Cruz took her to his room in his arms, because her legs were too wobbly to hold her up. She'd buried her face in his shoulder, eyes closed, weakly trying to block out the storm that had just passed but had left her reeling and trembling.

Her head hurt after too many confessions and an over-load of pleasure. And too many questions that she didn't want to answer now. Or ever, maybe.

His room was dark and austere. There was a four-poster bed with elaborate drapes. This was very evidently the old part of the *castillo*.

He put her down on the side of his bed and she felt shell-shocked when he disappeared into what she presumed to be the bathroom. She heard the sound of running water and a few minutes later he appeared again and took her into the en-suite.

The bath smelled amazing. Like Cruz. Musky and ex-otic. He helped her out of her dishevelled clothes and into the hot water. She sank down and looked at him warily. He wore nothing but his jeans, slung low on his hips. She wished she had the nerve to ask him to join her, but she also wanted time to herself, to try and take in everything without him scrambling her brain to pieces.

As if reading her mind, he said, 'I'll be waiting outside,' and walked out, leaving her alone with thoughts she suddenly didn't want to think about.

Coward. She wanted to sink down under the water and block everything out, but she couldn't.

She let out a long, shuddering breath. It really was as if a storm had taken place down in Cruz's study, whip-ping everything up and then incinerating it in the fire that had blown up between them, white-hot and devas-tating. But a very fragile sense of peace stole over her as she lay there, even as she had to acknowledge that she wasn't sure where she stood now. And wasn't sure if she wanted to find out.

Aware that the water was cooling rapidly, and Cruz was waiting, she washed perfunctorily, stiffening as a jolt of sensation went through her when she touched the tenderness between her legs.

When she finally emerged, in a voluminous towelling robe with the sleeves rolled up her arms, Cruz was standing at the window. He turned around and she could see that he'd changed into dark trousers and a long-sleeved top and his hair was damp. So he'd gone to another room to shower. Because he'd wanted to give her space, or because he couldn't bear to spend more time with her?

Trinity gritted her jaw against the sudden onset of paranoia.

He came forward. 'How are you?'

She nodded. 'I'm okay.'

He was looking at her with a strange expression on his face, as if he'd never seen her before. In spite of the explosive intimacies they'd just shared Trinity felt as if a chasm yawned between them now.

'I'm sorry,' she said impulsively, thinking of the look on his face when she'd revealed the depth of Rio's hatred.

A muscle ticked in Cruz's jaw. 'You're sorry? For what? It's me who should be apologising to you for all but forcing you into this marriage, and for what my brother put you through to get back at me.'

His belief in her innocence didn't make her feel peaceful now—it made her feel sick. If he really believed that she had just been a pawn in Rio's game what future was there for them? Her heart lurched. *None.* Because he had to be regretting this marriage, which had been born out of an erroneous belief that he couldn't trust her and that he needed to protect his nephews.

It was the last question she wanted to ask, but she had to. 'What happens now?'

He smiled, but it was mirthless. 'What happens now? What happens now is that you could be pregnant. We didn't use protection.' He cursed volubly. 'I didn't even think of it.'

Trinity sank down onto the side of the bed nearest to her as her legs gave way. 'Neither did I,' she said faintly. She'd felt it...the hot rush of his release inside her...and she'd conveniently blocked it out.

She stared at Cruz's grim countenance as the significance of this sank in. The full, horrifying significance.

If she was pregnant then he wouldn't be able to disentangle himself from this marriage—and she didn't need to be psychic to intuit that that was exactly what he wanted. He was angry.

'There was two of us there,' she pointed out, feeling sick. 'It wasn't just your oversight.'

His mouth twisted. 'As much as I appreciate your sentiment, I was the one who should have protected you.'

You. Not *us*.

Panic galvanised Trinity at the prospect of Cruz resenting her for ever for a moment of weakness.

She calculated swiftly and stood up. 'I'm sure I'm not pregnant. It's a safe time for me. And even if it happened, by some miracle, it doesn't mean anything. We don't have to stay married—we could work something out.'

'That,' Cruz said coolly, fixing his amber gaze on her, 'would never be an option in a million years. If you are pregnant then we stay married.'

'But if I'm not...?'

'Then we will discuss what happens. But for now we wait. I have to go to Madrid again in two weeks. I'll set up an appointment with my doctor and we'll go together. That should be enough time for a pregnancy test to show up positive or negative...'

Feeling numb, Trinity said, 'We could just wait. I'll know for sure in about three weeks.'

Cruz shook his head. 'No, we'll find out as soon as possible.'

Trinity really hated the deeply secret part of her that hoped that she might be pregnant, because that was the only way she knew she'd get to stay in Cruz's life. But if she wasn't… The sense of desolation that swept over her was so acute that she gabbled something incoherent and all but ran out of the room to return to hers.

Cruz didn't come after her, or try to stop her, which told her more eloquently than words ever could how he really felt about her.

Cruz stood in the same spot for a long time, looking at the door. He'd had to let Trinity go, even though it had taken nearly everything he possessed not to grab her back. But he couldn't—not now. Not after the most monumental lapse in control he'd ever experienced.

He started to pace back and forth. He'd fallen on her in his study like a caveman. Wild. Insatiable. Filled with such a maelstrom of emotions that the only way he'd known how to avoid analysing them was to sink inside her and let oblivion sweep them away. But he couldn't avoid it now.

He'd been angry with her for revealing the extent of Rio's antipathy—but hadn't he known all along, really? And she'd just been the reluctant messenger.

He'd felt anger at himself for indulging in that delusion in a bid to forge some meagre connection with his only family. And he'd felt anger that Trinity had been so abused by Rio *and* him. He hadn't deserved her purity and innocence after all he'd put her through, and yet she'd given it to him with a sensuality and abandon that still took his breath away.

He stopped. Went cold. He'd actually had a tiny moment of awareness just before he'd come that there was no protection. But he'd been so far gone by then that to have pulled away from Trinity's clasping heat would have killed him… Cruz knew that there was no other woman on this earth who would have had that effect on him.

The insidious suspicion took root… Had he subconsciously wanted to risk getting her pregnant? Because he was aware that after what she'd told him he could no longer insist they stay married if she was innocent of everything he'd thrown at her?

Cruz sank down heavily on the end of the bed. If that was what had happened then he was an even sicker bastard than Rio.

When he thought of how he'd treated Trinity…how he'd shoved the past down her throat at every opportunity without giving her a chance to defend herself or explain…he deserved for her to walk away without a second glance.

But if she was pregnant then she would stay. And Cruz would be aware every day of his life that he had trapped her for ever.

That moment when she'd said so emotionally, *'I don't want to tell you because I don't want to hurt you,'* came back to him. Its full impact.

The fact that she'd actually been willing to keep it from him—the full extent of Rio's ambition and hatred—made him feel even worse. At best she pitied him. At worst she would come to resent him, just as Rio had, if she was pregnant and had no choice but to stay…

By the time Trinity came down for breakfast with the boys the following morning, feeling hollow and tired, she knew that Cruz was no longer in the *castillo*. And sure enough Julia appeared with a note for her.

I have to go to Madrid for a couple of days and then New York. I'll return in time for the doctor's appointment. Cruz.

It couldn't be more obvious that he didn't want to have anything to do with her until they knew if she was pregnant and then he would *deal* with it.

Even Mrs Jordan seemed to sense that something was going on, because she kept shooting Trinity concerned looks. She did her best to project as happy a façade as possible, and suggested that Mrs Jordan take the opportunity to go to Scotland for a few days to see her son, telling her that she'd just need her back for when she would be going to Madrid.

She also, if she was honest, wanted time alone with the boys to lick her wounds.

She filled their days with activities, wearing herself and the boys out so comprehensively that she could sleep. But that didn't stop the dreams, which now featured her running through the *castillo*, going into every room, endlessly searching for Cruz.

And each night before she went to sleep she forced herself to remember what he'd said in London, when she'd asked him about marrying for love: *'I have no time for such emotions or weaknesses...'*

Two weeks later...

Trinity was standing on Harley Street, having just come out of the doctor's office, in the bright spring sunshine. Cruz had brought her to London instead of Madrid at the last minute, because there had been something urgent he had to attend to at the UK bank.

She felt raw now, being back here. Where it had all started. And she felt even more raw after her appointment with the doctor...

A sleek car pulled up just then, and stopped. Trinity saw a tall figure uncoil from the driver's seat. *Cruz.* He'd timed his meeting so that he could meet her after the doctor's appointment.

He held the passenger door open for her to get in, saying nothing as she did so, just looking at her carefully. When he was behind the wheel he looked at her again.

Feeling too brittle at that moment, Trinity said, 'I'll tell you when we get to the house.'

They were staying overnight.

A muscle pulsed in Cruz's jaw, but he said nothing and just drove off. Trinity felt a little numb as she watched the streets go by outside, teeming with people engrossed in their daily lives.

When they got to the Holland Park house her sense of déjà-vu was overwhelming. The door closed behind them, echoing in the cavernous hall. Trinity's heart was thumping and she could feel clammy sweat breaking out on her skin. She sensed Cruz behind her, watching her, waiting, and slowly turned around.

She knew she had to say the words. She opened her mouth and prayed to sound cool and in control. Not as if she was breaking apart inside. She looked at him.

'I'm not pregnant, Cruz.'

He said nothing for a long moment. Trinity was expecting to see relaxation in the tense lines of his body. Eventually he said, 'We should talk, then.'

She recoiled at the thought of doing it right now. 'Can we do it later, please? I'm quite tired.'

Cruz nodded once. 'Of course. Whenever you're ready. I'll be in my study.'

'Okay,' Trinity said faintly, and turned to go up the stairs to the bedrooms. Calling herself a coward as she did so. She was just staying the execution. That was all.

CHAPTER TEN

AFTERNOON PASSED INTO dusk and evening outside Cruz's study, but he was oblivious. Two words echoed in his head: *not pregnant...not pregnant.* He'd felt an unaccountably shocking sense of loss. When he had no right.

Trinity would get pregnant one day, and create the family she'd always wanted. And she deserved that. There was no reason for him not to let her go now. If anything, *he had to.* It was time for him to make reparation.

It had come far too belatedly—the realisation that Rio's deep hatred of Cruz hadn't irreparably damaged his ability to care. That his mother's even deeper cynicism hadn't decimated the tiny seed of hope he'd believed to have been crushed long ago—hope for a different kind of life, one of emotional fulfilment and happiness. One not bound by duty and destiny and a desire to protect himself from emotional vulnerability at all costs.

He'd never wanted more because he'd never really known what that was. Until he'd seen Trinity interact so lovingly and selflessly with his nephews and had found himself sitting up in their room all night, watching them sleep and vowing to slay dragons if he had to, to keep them safe.

The thought of family had always been anathema to him, but now—

He heard a sound and looked up to see his door open. *Trinity.* She'd changed and was wearing soft faded jeans and a long cardigan, which she'd pulled around herself. Her hair was down and a little mussed, and her face was bare of make-up. Her feet were bare too.

For a second Cruz thought he might be hallucinating... even though she wasn't wearing the same clothes as that night... Past and present were meshing painfully right now. Mocking him with the brief illusory fantasy that perhaps there could be such a thing as a second chance.

He stood up as she came in and shut the door behind her.

Her voice was husky. 'I'm sorry. I slept far later than I wanted to.'

On automatic pilot, Cruz asked, 'Are you hungry? Do you want to eat?'

She shook her head and smiled, but it was tight. 'No, thanks—no appetite.'

A bleakness filled Cruz. No doubt she just wanted to sort this out and be gone. Back to the life he'd snatched out of her hands.

'Please, sit down.'

Again, so polite. Trinity came in and sat down. The weight of their history in this room was oppressive. She'd told a white lie about sleeping—she hadn't slept a wink all afternoon, was too churned up. She'd spent most of her time pacing up and down.

After an initial acute sense of loss that she wasn't pregnant she'd felt a sense of resolve fill her. She wasn't going to give up without a fight. She knew Cruz had an innate sense of honour and decency, so even if that was all she had to work with she would.

Cruz sat down. His shirt was open at the top and his shirtsleeves were rolled up.

'You said that part of the deal with Rio was that he would pay for you to do a degree?'

Trinity blinked, taken by surprise that he'd remembered that. 'Yes, he did.'

'Do you still want to do it?'

She felt as if she was in an interview. 'Well, I haven't had much time to think about it lately, but yes...at some point I think I'd like to.'

Cruz nodded. 'I'll make sure you get a chance to do your degree, Trinity, wherever you want to do it.'

'Cruz...' She trailed off, bewildered. 'I presumed we were going to talk about what happens next—not my further education and career options.'

His voice was harsh. 'That is what happens next. You get to get on with your life—the life you would have had if you hadn't had the misfortune to meet me and my brother.'

He stood up then, and walked to the window which overlooked the park. It was still light outside—just.

Trinity stood up too, anger starting to sizzle. 'You do not get to do this, Cruz—blame yourself for what happened. Even Rio can't be apportioned blame either...not really.'

She came around the desk and stood a few feet away from him.

'I was just as much to blame. I shouldn't have been so hurt after what had happened between us that I spilled my guts to Rio with the slightest encouragement. You might not have handled it very well, but you didn't take any liberty I wasn't willing to give. It was the most thrilling moment of my life up to that point.'

Cruz turned around. Trinity saw his gaze drop and widen, and colour darken his cheeks. She didn't have to look down to know that her cardigan had fallen open, revealing her flimsy vest top and braless breasts underneath. She could feel her nipples peak under his gaze, and her heart thumped hard. She couldn't deny that she'd hoped to provoke a reaction from him.

'And there's this, Cruz.' She gestured between them, where tension crackled. 'This hasn't gone away...has it?'

His gaze rose and his jaw clenched. 'It's not about that any more. It's about you getting a divorce and moving on.'

Divorce.

Trinity's heart started thumping. She pulled the cardigan around herself again, feeling exposed. 'I told you before that I won't abandon Matty and Sancho—that hasn't changed.'

Cruz's voice was tight. 'The fact that you stepped in and protected and nurtured my nephews went above and beyond the call of duty.'

Trinity felt even more exposed now. 'I told you—I explained why—'

'I know,' Cruz said, and the sudden softness in his voice nearly killed her. 'But they're not really your responsibility. You have a life to live. And I won't be responsible for stopping you. We can work out a custody arrangement. I wouldn't stop you from being in their lives. But they're in good hands now.'

For a second Trinity wondered how she was still standing...how she wasn't in a broken heap at Cruz's feet. Whatever pain she'd experienced in her life didn't come close to the excruciating agony she felt right now.

Yet something dogged deep within her forced her to ask hoarsely, 'Do *you* want a divorce, Cruz?'

His eyes were burning. 'I want you to have your life back, Trinity. And I will support you and your relationship with the boys however you want.'

She folded her arms across her chest and Cruz's gaze dropped again to where the swells of her breasts were pushed up. Something came to life in her blood and belly. The tiniest kernel of *hope*.

'You didn't answer me. Do *you* want a divorce?'

His eyes met hers and she saw something spark deep in their golden depths before it faded. Something cold skated across her skin. A sense of foreboding.

'What I want,' Cruz bit out, 'is for my life to return to where it was before I ever met you.'

Trinity looked at him blankly for a long moment. And then, as his words impacted like physical blows, she sucked in a pained breath. Her fight drained away and her arms dropped heavily to her sides.

She might have fought Cruz if she'd thought there was half a chance. But there wasn't. He wanted her to have her life back. But he wanted his back too. She'd been a fool to think they had a chance. To think that she could persuade him by seducing him…

She whirled around to leave, terrified he'd see how badly he'd hurt her. The door was a blur in her vision as she reached for the knob, just wanting to escape.

She heard a movement behind her and then Cruz said hoarsely, 'Stop. Do not walk out through that door, Trinity.'

Her hand was on the knob. Her throat was tight, her vision blurring. She wouldn't turn around. 'Why?' she asked rawly.

His voice came from much closer. He sounded broken. 'Because I let you go through it once before and it was the worst mistake of my life.'

He put his hands on her shoulders and turned her around. She didn't want him to see the emotion on her face. But this was Cruz, who demanded and took, so he tipped her face up and cursed.

She looked at him and her heart flip-flopped. The stark mask was gone and he was all emotion. Raw emotion. And it awed her—because she realised now how adept he'd been at holding it all back for so long.

He'd been so controlled. But no more.

'I'm sorry,' he said, cupping her face, thumbs wiping at tears she hadn't even realised were falling. 'I didn't mean what I just said. It was cruel and unforgivable. I only said it because in that split second I thought going back to the life I had before I knew you was preferable to the pain of opening up. I thought I was doing the right thing…forcing you out of my life…'

Trinity whispered brokenly, 'I don't want you to force me out of your life.'

Cruz's whole body tensed. 'Do you mean that?'

She nodded, heart thumping. She put her hands on his and repeated her question. 'What do you want, Cruz?'

His eyes glowed with a new light. He said roughly, 'I want you. For ever. Because I know there can never be anyone else for me. I want to stay married to you and I want a chance to show you how sorry I am—for everything.'

Trinity just stared at him. Wondering if she was hallucinating.

He went on. 'I want to create a family with you—the kind of family neither of us had. Nor Rio. Maybe through his sons we can give him that finally. But,' he said, 'if you want a divorce...if you want to walk away...then I won't stop you. As much as I wanted you to be pregnant, I'm happy you aren't because I couldn't have borne knowing that you'd never had a choice... Now you do have a choice.'

Trinity's vision blurred again. 'I choose you, Cruz. I would always choose you.'

'I love you,' Cruz said fervently.

Trinity blinked back her tears and sucked in a shuddering breath. 'I came down here this evening prepared to fight and make you see, and then you said—'

Cruz stopped her mouth with his in a long soulful kiss. When they broke apart they were both breathing heavily, and Trinity realised that her back was against the wall of shelves. Cruz's body was pressed against hers, the unmistakable thrust of his arousal turning her limbs to jelly and her blood into fire. With an intent look on his starkly beautiful face he pushed her cardigan off her shoulders and pulled it off.

Euphoria made Trinity's heart soar. 'What are you doing?'

But Cruz was busy pulling down the straps of her vest top and exposing her breasts to his hungry gaze. Hoarsely he said, 'I'm taking care of unfinished business—if that's all right?'

As he made short work of undoing her jeans and pulling them down excitement mounted, and she said breathily, 'I have no objections.' She kicked her jeans off completely.

Cruz stopped for a moment and looked at her, all teasing and sexy seductiveness gone as the significance of the moment impacted on them. 'I love you.'

Trinity nodded, biting her lip to stave off more emotion. 'I love you too...'

But then their urgency to connect on a deeper level took over again.

Cruz stepped out of his clothes. She reached up and wound her arms around his neck, revelling in the friction of her body against his, and when Cruz picked her up she wrapped her legs tight around his hips and together they finished what they'd started, soaring high enough to finally leave the past behind and start again.

EPILOGUE

'CAREFUL, BOYS, YOUR little sister is not a doll,' Cruz admonished Matty and Sancho, who were tickling their four-month-old sister where she lay in her pram in the shade. The fact that she was their cousin and not really their sister was something they could wrap their heads around when they were older.

The boys giggled and ran away, chasing each other down the lawn, dark heads gleaming in the sunlight.

Cruz watched them go. They'd grown so much in the two years since he and Trinity had officially adopted them—turning their legal guardianship into something much more permanent and binding.

One day, not long after the adoption had come through, they'd both suddenly started calling him Papa. As if they'd taken a private mutual consultation to do so. The day it had happened he'd looked at Trinity, unable to keep the emotion from filling his eyes and chest. She'd reached out and taken his hand, her eyes welling up too as they'd realised what had just happened.

They were a family.

He shook his head now, marvelling that he couldn't even remember a time before these two small boys existed. He would die for them. It was that simple. It was bittersweet to know that he was finally able to show his love for Rio by protecting and nurturing his nephews like this.

A happy gurgle made Cruz look down again to see his daughter, Olivia—who was already being called Livvy—smiling gummily and waving her arms and legs. She had the bright blue eyes of her mother and a tuft of golden curls on her head, and she had Cruz so wrapped around her tiny finger that he could only grin like a loon and bend down to pick her up.

'Hey,' protested a sleepy voice, 'you're meant to be getting her to sleep.'

Cruz looked to where Trinity was lying in a gently rocking hammock between two trees. Her hair was loose and long around her shoulders and she was wearing short shorts and a halterneck top that showed off her lightly golden skin and luscious curves. An indulgent smile made her mouth curve up, telling Cruz that he was *so* busted where his baby daughter was concerned.

Whatever he felt for his children expanded tenfold every time he looked at this woman, who filled his heart and soul with such profound grace and love he was constantly awed by it.

In spite of their busy lives she was already one year into a three-year degree in business and economics at the University of Seville, and loving it.

The *castillo* was almost unrecognisable too, having undergone a massive renovation and redecoration. Now it was bright and airy, with none of the darkness of its tainted past left behind.

Cruz devoured her with his eyes as he walked over, holding his precious bundle close. Trinity's cheeks flushed as their eyes met and desire zinged between them. Ever-present. Everlasting.

She made room for him on the family-sized hammock and then settled under the arm he put behind her, her hand over Livvy where she was now sleeping on his chest, legs and arms sprawled in happy abandon.

The boys were shouting in the distance—happy sounds. Cruz could hear Mrs Jordan's voice, so he knew they were being watched. He took advantage of the brief respite and tugged Trinity closer into his chest. She looked up at him, her mouth still turned up in a smile that was halfway between innocent and devilishly sexy.

Emotion gripped him, as it so often did now, but instead of avoiding it he dived in. 'Thank you,' he said, with a wealth of meaning in his words.

Thank you for giving him back his heart and an emotional satisfaction he would never have known if he hadn't met her and fallen in love.

And even though he didn't say those words he didn't have to, because he could see from the sudden brightness in her eyes that she knew exactly what he meant.

She reached up and touched her lips to his—a chaste kiss, but with a promise of so much more. And she whispered emotionally against his mouth, 'I love you, Cruz. Always.'

'Always,' he whispered back, twining his fingers with hers where they rested over their daughter.

Trinity rested her head in the spot made for her, between his chin and his shoulder, and the future stretched out before them, full of love and endless days just like this one.

* * * * *

If you enjoyed this story,
why not explore these other great reads
from Abby Green

MARRIED FOR THE TYCOON'S EMPIRE
AWAKENED BY HER DESERT CAPTOR
AN HEIR FIT FOR A KING

And don't miss these other
WEDLOCKED! *themed stories*

BRIDE BY ROYAL DECREE
by Caitlin Crews
BOUND BY HIS DESERT DIAMOND
by Andie Brock

Available now!

MILLS & BOON®
MODERN™

POWER, PASSION AND IRRESISTIBLE TEMPTATION

A sneak peek at next month's titles...

In stores from 9th March 2017:

- **The Italian's One-Night Baby** – Lynne Graham
- **Once a Moretti Wife** – Michelle Smart
- **The Secret Heir of Alazar** – Kate Hewitt
- **His Mistress with Two Secrets** – Dani Collins

In stores from 23rd March 2017:

- **The Desert King's Captive Bride** – Annie West
- **The Boss's Nine-Month Negotiation** – Maya Blake
- **Crowned for the Drakon Legacy** – Tara Pammi
- **The Argentinian's Virgin Conquest** – Bella Frances

Just can't wait?
Buy our books online before they hit the shops!
www.millsandboon.co.uk

Also available as eBooks.

MILLS & BOON®

EXCLUSIVE EXTRACT

Stefano Moretti wants only revenge from his wife,
Anna. When she reappears after leaving him, with no
memory of their marriage, he realizes that this is his
chance…for a red-hot private seduction, followed by a
public humiliation! Until Stefano realizes there's
something he wants more than vengeance—Anna,
back in his bed for good!

Read on for a sneak preview of
ONCE A MORETTI WIFE

Stefano pressed his thumb to her chin and gently stroked
it. 'When your memories come back you will know the
truth. I will help you find them.'

Her heart thudding, her skin alive with the sensation
of his touch, Anna swallowed the moisture that had filled
her mouth.

When had she given in to the chemistry that had always
been there between them, always pulling her to him? She'd
fought against it right from the beginning, having no intention of joining the throng of women Stefano enjoyed such
a legendary sex life with. To be fair, she didn't have any
evidence of what he actually got up to under the bedsheets;
indeed it was something she'd been resolute in *not*
thinking about, but the steady flow of glamorous, sexy
women in and out of his life had been pretty damning.

When had she gone from liking and hugely admiring

him but with an absolute determination to never get into bed with him, to marrying him overnight? She'd heard of whirlwind marriages before but from employee to wife in twenty-four hours? Her head hurt just trying to wrap itself around it.

Had Stefano looked at her with the same glimmer in his green eyes then as he was now? Had he pressed his lips to hers or had she been the one...?

'How will you help me remember us?' she asked in a whisper.

His thumb moved to caress her cheek and his voice dropped to a murmur. 'I will help you find again the pleasure you had in my bed. I will teach you to become a woman again.'

Mortification suffused her, every part of her anatomy turning red.

I will teach you to be a woman again?

His meaning was clear. He knew she was a virgin.

Anna's virginity was not something she'd ever discussed with anyone. Why would she? Twenty-three-year-old virgins were rarer than the lesser-spotted unicorn. For Stefano to know that...

Dear God, it was *true*.

All the denial she'd been storing up fell away.

She really had married him.

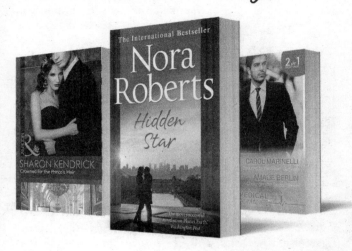

Join Britain's BIGGEST Romance Book Club

50% OFF your first parcel

- **EXCLUSIVE offers** every month

- **FREE delivery direc** to your door

- **NEVER MISS a title**

- **EARN Bonus Book** points

Call Customer Services
0844 844 1358*

or visit
millsandboon.co.uk/subscription